Jackson Jones
The Tale of a Boy, a Troll, and a Rather Large Chicken

ZONDERKIDZ

Jackson Jones: The Tale of a Boy, a Troll, and a Rather Large Chicken
Copyright © 2011 by Jennifer Kelly
Illustrations © 2011 by Ariane Elsammak

This title is also available as a Zondervan ebook.
Visit www.zondervan.com/ebooks.

Requests for information should be addressed to:

Zonderkidz, *Grand Rapids, Michigan 49530*

Library of Congress Cataloging-in-Publication Data

Kelly, Jennifer, 1973–
    Jackson Jones : the tale of a boy, a troll, and a rather large chicken / written by
Jenn Kelly ; illustrated by Ariane Elsammak.
        p.   cm.
    Summary: In the middle of a tremendous storm, ten-year-old Jackson Jones
finds himself in an immense tree, leading to more inexplicable adventures.
        ISBN 978-0-310-72293-9 (hardcover)
    1. Adventure and adventurers—Fiction. 2. Humorous stories. I. Elsammak,
Ariane, ill. II. Title.
PZ7.K29622Jab 2011
[Fic]—dc23   2011014464

Art direction: Sarah Molegraaf
Cover design: Ariane Elsammak
Interior design: Carlos Estrada
Interior composition: Greg Johnson/Textbook Perfect

Printed in the United States of America

11 12 13 14 15 16 /DCI/ 23 22 21 20 19 18 17 16 15 14 13 12 11 10 9 8 7 6 5 4 3 2 1

Jackson Jones
The Tale of a Boy, a Troll, and a Rather Large Chicken

written by
Jenn Kelly

illustrated by
Ariane Elsammak

ZONDERVAN.com/
AUTHORTRACKER
follow your favorite authors

Other Books by Jenn Kelly:

*Jackson Jones: The Tale of a Boy, an Elf,
and a Very Stinky Fish* (book 1)

*Jackson Jones: The Tale of a Boy, a Troll,
and a Rather Large Chicken* (book 2)

To God, Danny, and Jackson.
My life, my love, and my heart.

Table of Contents

No squirrels were harmed in the creation of this book. Honest.

Which Is Extremely Stinky

Another bag of garbage.

Rotting, smelly, festering garbage. With holes in the bag. So it would leak.

And here he was, without a wheelbarrow. Or a donkey. Or a super cool, industrial four-wheeler.

So Stimple sighed again, hefted the rotting, smelly, festering garbage bag onto his back with a squashy splat, and began to pick his nose.

Which Is an Absolute Tragedy
(Prepare Your Handkerchiefs!)

Jackson was furious.

It was *not* fair.

It was *not* his fault.

He seethed as he stomped outside, pounding his feet as hard as he could against the kitchen floor, then slammed the door shut.

He growled as he walked over to the pool and picked up the net.

"Not my fault... Why am I the one getting in trouble?" he muttered.

Jackson fumed as he remembered what had happened. He had run up the stairs to his room to grab his notebook because he had a *great* idea for a story. He opened his bedroom door and there was his little brother, giggling, sitting on the floor and clutching a magic marker. And Jackson's heart fell into his stomach.

His brother had doodled all over his notebook.

Jackson snatched the book from his hands, ignoring his brother's wails. "What are you doing?" he yelled.

Jackson opened the notebook.

Every single page was ruined.

Doodles and scribblings on every page. Cross-outs and thick lines, scratching out what Jackson had written.

His stories were ruined.

"You. are. such. a. BRAT!" Jackson screamed.

His little brother's bottom lip stuck out and his eyes filled with tears. His mouth opened wide as he inhaled loudly.

"Stop ..." Jackson began. But he was interrupted by the siren that came rushing out of his little brother's mouth. He turned and ran crying down the hallway to his mother's room. Jackson followed angrily, his ruined notebook in hand.

"He's only five. He doesn't really know what he's doing, Jackson," his mom said gently, holding his little brother on her lap.

"He ruined my stories!" Jackson spluttered.

"I know he did, and I'm very sorry for that. But you should have put your notebook away, where he couldn't find it. You need to keep things out of sight. You know how curious he is," his mother said.

Jackson turned and whipped his notebook across the room. It hit the wall with a *THWACK* and then slid to the floor. Jackson felt better. For a moment.

"I think you need to cool off before we finish talking," said Mrs. Jones. "You can cool off cleaning out the pool."

3

In Which There Are Dragons.
Sort of.

Jackson was in an extremely rotten mood. Such a rotten mood, in fact, that he didn't notice the way the sun glimmered off the water in the pool, the way the wind whistled through his hair, the songs the birds were singing ... No, wait. The birds weren't singing. That was odd.

But Jackson was in such a rotten mood that he didn't even notice that the birds were silent. He picked up the pool net, brandishing it like a shining sword that would slice right into a dragon's chest.

"Aha! Take that!" Jackson swung his mighty sword and slashed the dragon, splashing himself with pool water in the process.

He looked down at his grubby shorts and T-shirt, scowling. Then he laughed. Then scowled again. He was supposed to be in a rotten mood, after all. Jackson swirled the pool net in the water to remove fallen bits of twigs and leaves. A big black bug clung to the net. "Get off!" Jackson shook it.

And then he shivered, because all of a sudden the sun had disappeared behind a very big, very gray cloud. Better move faster. His ten-and-a-half-year-old arms pumped while he shoveled out more debris. (*Debris* is a fancy name for garbage.)

Ouch!

Jackson looked down at his arm. Something had stung him, but he didn't see anything.

Ouch! Jackson felt his head. Nothing there. But that hurt! Jackson backed up, looking around for wasps. No, there didn't seem to be any. But ... ouch! Jackson looked up to the sky and was hit right in the nose.

Hail!

Little round-ish balls of ice, some of them the size of marbles, zoomed down from the sky, smashing into the backyard and splashing into the pool. Jackson chucked the net, covered his head with his arms, and ran toward the shed. He peeked out the window and watched the hail fall.

What a strange day.

Jackson pressed his nose harder to the window, squeezed his eyes tight, and wondered if there was something different in the air.

But all he could smell was the dank smell of soil hanging in the air. (*Dank* means moist and wet. Not wet like your dog's nose, but like a gardening shed full of new soil.)

Hail was really coming down now. Loud *thunks* hit the roof and large *plops* splashed into the pool. Little white balls covered every surface. And then Jackson's eyes caught something that was most certainly not hail.

The patio umbrella was still set up beside the pool! The hail smashed against the purple-and-green-striped umbrella, threatening to tear the fabric. Jackson threw his weight against the door, struggling against the howling wind that pushed back against it. Finally, — finally — it creaked open and Jackson slipped out. He threw his hands over his face, trying to see through the falling miniature cannonballs.

No, they were like little blasts of fireballs. Mini fireballs blasting out of the dragon's mouth. He would have to fight through them! He had to save the village from this iniquitous beast! (*Iniquitous* means super-duper nasty.) Jackson recovered his pool net and sliced it through the air and let out an impressive battle cry.

"Aaaaaaah—OUCH!" A fireball hit him in the back. He ducked and dodged, narrowly avoiding the blazes of hot fire that would burn right through his armor. The wind pushed itself against him and his legs strained with the weight. But just as he grabbed the umbrella pole and reached up inside for the latch, a sharp burn pierced his leg. He was hit! But he had to go on. He had to continue—even if he died! He dropped his pool-net sword and fumbled with the latch. Bruises were popping up between his goose bumps. The wind pushed the umbrella up, threatening to pull it out of his hands. He gripped harder and clenched his teeth.

"You can do this!" he whispered fiercely to himself. "For honor! For glory! For the kingdom!" He forced his hand up and grasped the latch, giving it a yank.

It was stuck!

The wind snapped at Jackson's legs, trying to knock him over. His numb fingers squeezed the button and, at that very moment, a gust of wind blew so hard up into the umbrella that Jackson was lifted off the ground.

Jackson gripped the pole even tighter, and a strong north wind blew Jackson and the umbrella over onto the ground. He landed hard on his shoulder.

And just at that moment, just as Jackson sat back up, the wind picked up, filling the umbrella with air. Jackson's feet dragged along the ground, and then he was airborne.

He held tight, praying his weight would keep him from flying away.

But it didn't—Jackson was still scrawny—and he flew up into the sky.

In Which You Think This Is *The Wizard of Oz*, but It Isn't

Jackson's eyes were getting dizzy from all the purple and green stripes spinning in front of him. The umbrella swished and popped as the wind pushed them along, faster and faster. Jackson swallowed and told himself not to look down.

He looked down.

He had to be at least thirty feet in the air! Should he let go? Jackson flew over the large, thorny rose-bush garden in the community park.

Uh, maybe not.

The wind blew and blew, while Jackson's legs dangled helplessly in the air. If you were to stand back and look, you would see a large patio umbrella with crazy purple-and-lime-green stripes. And then you'd see a pair of little legs with sandals dangling in the wind. Up and down, up and down, the umbrella and Jackson flew. Jackson's arms began to ache. It was like climbing the ropes in gym class but not as embarrassing.

They were fifty feet up.

Where on earth were they going to land?

Jackson just held on. What else could he do?

chapter

5

In Which We Find Out Where
Jackson Is Going

Jackson's throat was raw from yelling for help. But it was no use. No one was outside and even if they were, the hail smashing to the ground and the blowing winds were making too much noise for him to be heard. His fingers ached and his arms felt like they were about to fall off. Jackson shut his eyes tightly as he blew higher and higher into the sky.

And then, entirely without warning, he crashed.

chapter

6

In Which We Have No Idea
Where Jackson Is

Jackson was thrust sharply upwards and he hit his head on one of the umbrella spokes. Ow! But at least he had stopped. Actually, he seemed to be stuck.

Jackson looked down. Just below his dangling feet was a tree branch. It was quite large—about fifteen feet across. Jackson slowly let go of the umbrella and dropped down onto the branch. He rubbed his sore arms, taking in his surroundings.

He was in a tree. A very large tree. Possibly the largest tree in the world. Hard to tell. Until you've seen every tree in the world, you really can't make outlandish claims like that. Limbs branched off in all directions, their green leaves casting a soothing glow. Jackson walked toward the end of the branch and almost fell over.

The forest went on for miles and miles. He was so far up that all he could see were the tops of the trees. Had he really been blown that far? He shook his head. Where was he?

Jackson turned and walked back along the branch. The striped umbrella was still stuck up in the tree. He sighed. And scratched his head. And then scratched his ... *ahem* ... behind. (It was itchy!) And then ...
THWACK!

In Which There Is a *Lot* of Thwacking

*T*HWACK!

"Ouch!" Jackson yelled, his eyes tearing and his forehead stinging from the pain.

"Oi! Oi! Gerr-off my tree!"

THWACK!

"Stop it! That hurts!" Jackson covered his head.

"Oh ho! Talk back, will ya? Take that!"

THWACK!

Jackson backed up, peeking between his arms.

A large, hairy creature gripped a monstrous fly swatter in his big, meaty fists. His furry face was purple with rage.

"Get outta my tree! Go find yer own!" he yelled, raising the monstrous fly swatter up in the air.

"Ack! Stop it! Let me explain!" Jackson backed up even farther, checking behind himself to make sure that he wasn't running out of branch.

"Humph! 'Splain nothing! I don't like no weirdo creatures in my tree! So get yer silly parasol and get outta my tree before I thwack ya again!" The purple-faced creature roared. (A *parasol* is like an umbrella, only prettier!)

"I'm no weird creature! You're the weird one, going around smacking people for no good reason!" Jackson's grayish-bluish-greenish-brownish eyes were still tearing up. He wiped them with the back of his hands so he could see better.

"No good reason? Ya whippersnapper! You're the one in my tree! Trespassing!" The creature gripped the fly swatter tighter and started toward Jackson.

"I'm not a whippersnapper! I've never snapped a whip in my life!" Jackson yelled, standing tall and trying to look tough. But since he still hadn't hit his growth spurt (that wouldn't happen for another two years), he wasn't doing a very good job.

Silence.

The creature's furry face turned blue. Jackson raised his fists. Just in case. And then he heard a very strange noise indeed. Jackson looked up and realized that the creature was laughing.

"*Baaaa hahahahahaha!* Never snapped a whip! Ha! That's a good one! I like you, boy!" And a meaty hand pounded Jackson's shoulder. *Ouch.* Jackson rubbed it gingerly. (Gingerly isn't a seasoning. Ginger is a seasoning, and it's delicious in cookies and stir-fry. *Gingerly* means, "Please touch gently, because *gosh* that hurts!")

"Can you please tell me where I am?" Jackson asked as politely as possible.

The creature wiped a tear from his furry eye. Not that his eyes were furry. But his thick, bushy brown eyebrows were, and they hung down into his eyes. "Cancha read, boy?"

Jackson looked around. "Read? Read what?"

He pointed at his chest. "This ain't English? Or whatever?"

On the creature's chest, pinned very neatly, was a sign. It read:

Stimple: Keeper of the Tree

"What's a Stimple?"

"I am!" The creature laughed. "I'm a tree-troll!" He pulled his work bag open and shoved his monstrous fly swatter inside. Jackson caught a glimpse of a few screws, a hammer, a wrapped up ball of something-or-other and a bottle of something slimy. And a roll of . . .

"Why do you carry around toilet paper?" Jackson asked.

Stimple glared at him, snapping his bag closed. "Nosy."

"But . . ."

"Why do *you* think I have toilet paper?" Stimple raised a hairy eyebrow.

Jackson swallowed and quickly changed the subject. Which was probably a good idea. We don't really want to know why Stimple had toilet paper or what he used it for, do we? We can guess on our own.

"So—ahem!—what does the Keeper of the Tree do?"

"I mind the tree." Stimple gave Jackson a strange look. Jackson nodded. (Wouldn't you?) "So what are ya doin' in my tree?" Stimple growled. His thick fingers twisted his bushy eyebrows as he approached Jackson.

Jackson explained how the wind had blown him away. (If you don't remember that part, go back a few pages and re-read. But really, you should pay better attention.)

Stimple nodded. "Hmm . . . hmm . . . well. Looks like we need to get you outta my tree. How 'bout you grab onto that parasol pole and I'll shove ya out and we'll let the wind take ya home!"

Jackson's eyeballs bugged out of his head. (Not literally.) "Um, is there a safer way to get out?"

Stimple frowned. Jackson could see that he was concentrating very, very hard. "Humph. I guess so. But I've got a lot of work to do first. You'll have to tag along."

"But couldn't you just tell me, and I'll go ahead and be on my way?" Jackson pleaded. "My family will be wondering where I am and why I haven't finished cleaning the pool."

Stimple turned away. "Your ... family? You? Have a family?" he whispered.

"Doesn't everyone?"

With a resounding snort, Stimple whirled around to face Jackson with red eyes. A growl came from his throat. "You'll help me with my chores, and then I'll get ya home."

"Okay! No problem. Not in a hurry. Happy to wait. Sorry to rush you," Jackson stammered, holding out his hand for Stimple to shake. Stimple stared at it.

"I don't know where that hand's been." Stimple turned away and began to scratch his nose.

The creature in front of Jackson was different, no doubt about it. Stimple was short, only coming up to Jackson's shoulders. He had a very large head and his ears were the size of saucers, (A *saucer* is a cute little plate for your teacup.) with long hairs sprouting off them. His eyes were tiny, so tiny you couldn't see what color they were. Actually, you probably could, but he was scowling so much that his eyes and bushy eyebrows were just lines. He wore a dark, dirty blazer and dark, dirty pants. He had a large nose, about the size of a sweet potato. And coming out of his sweet potato nose were two large tufts of hair. It looked like he had shoved two kittens up his nose. And below the two kittens shoved up his nose was a very huge beard. And it

30

seemed to have bits of this and that in it. Was that . . . was that a tortilla chip?

Stimple turned and plodded down the tree branch. Jackson followed, his arms straight out, trying to keep his balance.

"What? You gonna *fly* away?" Stimple roared with laughter. Jackson's face turned red, and he put his arms down.

And then he saw something most unexpected.

chapter 8

In Which Jackson Sees Something Most Unexpected

This is most unexpected," said Jackson. Because in front of them was a door.

And not just any door.

This was ...

... an elevator door.

chapter

9

In Which Stimple Does a Monkey Impression

Is that ... it can't be ... we're in a tree ..." Jackson spluttered.

Stimple snorted. "How else are ya supposed to get up and down? Swing like a monkey? Oo-oo-oo-eeee!" Stimple scratched his belly as he bounced, little bits of food flying from his beard. Jackson backed out of the way as an apple core fell from overhead and hit the ground.

"Erm ... you've dropped a few things," he said, pointing to the apple core and what looked like a half-eaten granola bar.

"Heh?" Stimple bent down and picked up the apple core and popped it in his mouth. Jackson turned away.

Jackson looked at the elevator door. It was made of wood (of course), and someone had carved lines of flowers and vines into the bark. Stimple's thick finger pushed the button beside it.

There was a whir and a churn and then ...

DING.

The door opened.

"Good morning, sir. Which floor, please?" asked a voice that was very serious, very dignified, and very polite.

Jackson's eyes popped out of his head.

Not literally.

chapter 10

In Which Jackson Meets an Old Friend

The gentleman in the elevator was old. White tufts of hair made little fluffy clouds around his ears. His expression was serious, but there was some kind of joke twinkling behind his dark blue eyes. He wore a dark maroon velvet suit with sparkling gold buttons and golden, tasseled epaulets. (*Epaulets* are like shoulder pads, but very fancy and official-looking.) A thick crease ran down the length of each of his pant legs, and his pants were tucked into a pair of red high-top sneakers.

"I know you! You're ... Sir Shaw! You ran the Book Room in my Great-Aunt Harriett's hair! What are you doing here?" Jackson exclaimed.

The elevator operator looked down at Jackson, his bushy white eyebrows almost covering his dark blue eyes. "I'm afraid I can't recall, sir. It's been a very long time since I worked in the Book Room." His eyes clouded a moment. "A very long time indeed." He

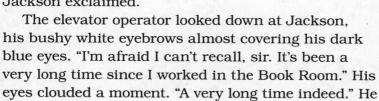

straightened himself. "Good morning, Stimple. Will you be coming in today? I would love to hear how you are are doing."

Stimple scowled. "No. I ain't ridin' in your elevator. Elevators are for you soft folk. I prefer the stairs." He pointed a thick finger at Jackson. "Go wait in the garden."

Jackson stepped inside, and with a whir and a churn, the door slid closed.

chapter 11

Which Begins Awkwardly but Gets Better After That

Jackson didn't know what to say. This was terribly awkward. Jackson stared at his shoes and twiddled his thumbs as Sir Shaw pulled the gold hand lever. It made little ticks as it changed gears. The elevator gave a little bump, and soon they were moving. A little black arrow above the door slowly moved downwards, counterclockwise. There weren't any numbers indicating which floor they were on, or which floor they were going to.

Sir Shaw stared straight ahead.

"Ahem!" Jackson cleared his throat. "How long ago did you switch jobs? I mean, were you promoted or something?" Jackson immediately wished he hadn't said anything. It probably wasn't a promotion, going from running a Book Room to running an elevator. Had Sir Shaw been demoted?

"I really cannot recall how long it has been," said Sir Shaw. "And no, I was not promoted *or* demoted. In my line of work, one goes where one is needed most." Sir Shaw's mouth gave a glimpse of a smile, but then it straightened back into a firm, serious line.

"What does that mean? Go where you're needed most?"

"Well, for example, I worked as a trapeze artist in a circus for a few years. After that I spent some time singing on cruise ships. And after that I toured with a famous opera star. But we will not get into that right now. One simply goes where one is needed. Which floor, sir?"

"Well," said Jackson slowly, "just where does this elevator go?"

"It goes up and it goes down."

Jackson rolled his eyes. "No, I mean, when the doors open, what happens?"

"Folks come in and folks go out."

"No! I mean, what's on each floor?"

Sir Shaw turned to look at Jackson, his dark blue eyes twinkling. "It is not for me to say. That is something you have to figure out yourself." Jackson sighed, but Sir Shaw just leaned in closer. "Stimple will be a while. Why not go on an adventure?"

Jackson's eyes widened. "But I have to get home. Maybe I could come back later?"

But then, with a whir and a churn ...

DING!

The elevator door opened.

chapter

12

In Which Jackson Is Well-Prepared

Jackson was looking out at a garden. Which doesn't make much sense, if you think about it. How could there be a garden in a tree? But after everything that has happened, you (as well as Jackson) are just better off accepting all these things that don't make sense. As a very famous author once wrote, "I've believed as many as six impossible things before breakfast." Just this morning, Jackson had believed that the crow in the backyard with the broken foot was actually a pirate's crow that had escaped to save his own life. But back to the garden.

You know those gardens that are tilled and maintained by seventeen full-time gardeners to be enjoyed briefly by a countess as she steps on her private balcony to breathe in the morning air before leaving to catch her private jet ride to Monaco? It was that kind of garden. But what made this garden even more amazing was that the entire garden was in a tree!

Jackson took a step when he felt a hand resting on his shoulder.

"You will need this, sir," the kind voice said. Sir Shaw's pristine, white-gloved hand held a leather satchel. Jackson looked at it, and then took it in his hands. He pulled the strap over his head and across his body, then started out the door once more.

"You might want to open the bag first," said Sir Shaw. "To see what is inside for your journey. Make sure you are well prepared."

Jackson flipped the top open. Inside the satchel were a heavy-duty flashlight, a bottle of water, and a roll of toilet paper.

"Toilet paper?" Jackson raised his eyebrows.

Sir Shaw shrugged. "You never know when you will need it."

"Um," Jackson began.

"Have a good day, sir."

And with a whir and a churn, the doors closed.

chapter

13

In Which Jackson Doesn't Get His Nap

The path that lay before Jackson was made of stepping stones. Creeping thyme grew between the stones, and tall lupines and bee balm led the way. Branches overhead had been trimmed back to make an archway. Jackson walked slowly and carefully along the path.

Up ahead was a gazebo. As Jackson's face lifted to catch the warm sun, he followed the path up and stepped inside. A hammock greeted him there, enticing him to lie down. He turned to sit when ...

... a dog bit his ... *ahem* ... behind.

In Which Jackson Finds Himself in a Pickle

Jackson jumped up and backed away from the hammock, his hands rubbing the sore spot.

A large, rather vicious-looking, black dog was glaring at him. Its dark eyes stared, unblinking, its teeth snarling and a large gob of saliva clinging to his upper lip. The dog panted heavily, then growled again, the hackles on his neck sharp and erect.

Jackson stepped back very, very slowly. "Easy, fella," he said. "Good boy, good boy . . . sit." The dog's muscular back legs walked forward as it lowered its head, growling from deep in its chest.

Jackson didn't know what to do. "Good boy. Easy. St—ay." The dog inched closer.

Jackson swallowed.

Oh, dear.

A Very Proper Introduction

Muffy! Manners!" a little voice squeaked.

Jackson's jaw dropped, and his eyes bugged out of his head. (Not literally.)

The creature in front of him was tiny, barely reaching Jackson's shoulders. Her hair was tucked neatly in a ponytail, and she wore a brown uniform, ironed perfectly with little creases where little creases should be. A red neckerchief was tied at her throat, and a leather pouch was fastened at her belted waist. Her big, long-lashed brown eyes fixed on Jackson, and she smiled.

"Are you here for the tour, sir?" her squeaky voice pipped.

"Meeka?"

chapter 16

There are Absolutely No Eels, Kangaroos, or Rhinoceroses in This Chapter

The elf in front of him batted her eyelashes and smiled uncertainly. "No, I am not Meeka. Meeka is my ... cousin." Her nose turned up a bit when she said Meeka's name.

"Cousin? You look so much like her!"

"Ah. Well. I think you'll find that *I* am tidy and organized while she is ... well, she's Meeka," said the elf. "Folks do seem to like her ..."

"I'll say! She gave me a tour of Great-Aunt Harriett's hair, and ..."

"Anyhow." The elf gave a mighty sniff. "I am Burt."

"Burt?"

She gave him a look. "Yes. Burt. Is that a problem?" The dog growled quietly. Burt shook her head and gave a very toothy smile. "Muffy, manners!" she sang. The dog sat back on its haunches.

"No, no. I think it's a great name!" Jackson watched Muffy. "I was worried that, uh, Muffy would rip my arm off! Ha!" Jackson gave a very nervous laugh.

Burt giggled. "Oh, no! He'd never do that! At least— he won't as long as I'm around. He's a great watchdog."

"Do you need a watchdog in here? I mean, we're in a *tree*." Jackson felt like he was pointing out the obvious.

Burt ruffled Muffy's fur with perfectly-polished, pink nails. "Yes, I do. He keeps out the eels and the kangaroos and the rhinoceroses."

"You get kangaroos up here?"

"I haven't seen any lately."

"That's because kangaroos don't climb trees!" Jackson said.

"Then Muffy's doing his job, isn't he? Yes, he is!" She rubbed his ears, her squeaky voice squeaking higher and higher.

Jackson shook his head. "Rhinoceroses can't climb trees. Neither can eels!"

Burt shrugged. "Well, it's nice to know I'm safe from eels and kangaroos and nasty-wasty rhinoceroses! Yes, I am!" she cooed. Muffy wagged his stumpy tail.

Jackson sighed. Who was this elf?

"So would you like a tour of the gardens?" She fluttered her eyelashes at him.

"Why not?" asked Jackson, shrugging his shoulders.

Burt straightened the already-straight hem of her skirt and patted her immaculate hair. She sniffed importantly and turned with a click of her heels. "We go this way."

In Which It Is Detrimental to Have Food in Your Pockets (Detrimental Means Yes, You Just Might Die)

The sun shone down, and Burt's little boots padded down the cobblestone path as she chatted.

"These are lupines. They were planted approximately fourteen hundred years ago. Every year I divide them and collect their seeds. These are sunflowers. I collect their seeds, too. This patch here is filled with annuals, so I have to till the ground and replant every spring."

Jackson whistled. Muffy's ears perked up and he growled. Jackson stopped walking.

Burt glanced at Jackson. "I wouldn't recommend whistling. Or clapping. Or making any sudden movements at all, really. And don't talk to him. He doesn't really like people. Or eels. Or kangaroos for that matter. Loathes rhinoceroses. He's highly trained to protect, you see." She patted his head, and Muffy thumped his stubby tail on the ground.

Burt looked up at Jackson suspiciously. "You don't have any food in your pockets, do you?"

Jackson shook his head.

Burt released a breath. "Good!" They kept walking.

"So . . ." said Jackson after a moment. "Do you take care of the garden all by yourself? I mean, does anyone else work here?"

Burt stopped walking and stared at Jackson. "Are you saying," she began in a steely voice. (*Steely* means very angry, but quiet—not that her voice was made of steel. But wouldn't it be cool if it was?) She stepped closer to him, her finger pointing at his chest like a weapon. "Are you saying that I am not capable of doing this job all by myself?"

Jackson jumped back. "No! No, of course not! I . . . it's just that this is such a big garden and you're so . . ."

"Small? That's what you were going to say, weren't you?" Her voice trilled upwards.

"No, that's not what I meant! I just meant that gardening is hard work!"

Burt sniffed and crossed her arms over her chest. "I'm sure you have no idea. This is the finest garden in the whole world. There could not possibly be another garden of such gorgeousness and beauty as this one. Could there?" she snarled.

"Ah, no, of course not." Jackson watched the hackles rise on Muffy's neck. He quickly averted his eyes and looked at the cobblestone path. It was incredibly tidy for a garden. "So, this is your job then?"

Burt patted her hair. (It was still immaculate.) "I have been given the very important job of minding the Author's garden."

Jackson started. "The Author? You work for the Author?"

Burt nodded.

"We *are* talking about the same Author? The one who created everything?"

She put a hand on her hip. "Duh." She examined her perfectly pink nails. "We need to continue with the tour now."

The path led to an arbor that was covered with climbing roses. Burt opened a little white gate and led Jackson on a path that circled around a white gazebo. Inside the gazebo were a black

wrought-iron table and two black wrought iron chairs. On top of the table was a red-and-white checkered table cloth with two place settings.

"This looks kind of familiar," Jackson murmured to himself as he walked toward a chair.

A death grip snatched his arm. Jackson stared at Burt in surprise.

"It's not for sitting," she hissed.

"I'm sorry?"

"No need to apologize. I'm sure you didn't know." Her snarl turned into a bright smile. Jackson suspected it was forced.

"Why can't I sit down?"

"Because you'll get it dirty."

"I'm sorry?"

"No need to apologize."

Jackson grunted in frustration. "Why would it get dirty? I'm not that dirty. And it's a chair. An *outside* chair!"

"Well . . ." Burt's voice trailed off as she looked him up and down. She sniffed disdainfully. "I'm sure you're a very nice boy and all, but I can't have you messing things up."

"Why is this table and chairs set up then?" he argued.

"So one can sit and eat a snack in the garden."

"Does anyone actually come and sit and eat a snack?" he asked.

Burt's laugh tinkled the air. "Of course not! Then it wouldn't be neat and pretty and perfect anymore! What a silly thing to do!"

"But we could sit down and have a snack, and I could help you clean up afterwards," said Jackson. "Aren't you hungry?"

"Or you could just not sit down and we'll continue with the tour and then you can go away," said Burt.

"What's the point of this being set up if you can't sit down?" Jackson's voice rose, his cheeks turning pink with frustration.

Muffy's hackles rose and he began to growl. Burt smiled sweetly at Jackson. "I'm sure you didn't mean to raise your voice at me. Muffy doesn't like it when my feelings are hurt. Does he, my little Muffy-puffy?" she sang.

Jackson sighed. "This is ridiculous."

"You just don't know what you're talking about. Only an ignoramus wouldn't understand why things have to be perfect here." (*Ignoramus* is what you call someone who clearly has no clue what's going on. But it's not really nice to call them that.) Burt patted Muffy's head and walked on.

Jackson was starting to get annoyed. Could you blame him? (His empty stomach probably wasn't helping his mood.) Burt was being ridiculously difficult. But some elves are just like that.

"Let's pretend I *am* an ignoramus. Why do things need to be perfect here? It's a very pretty garden, and aren't gardens for enjoying?" Jackson followed Burt down the path.

Burt raised her eyebrows. "The Author made this garden. He made the garden perfect. He made it to be *kept* perfect."

"What?"

Burt's hands began to wave in the air. "Because he's perfect! How can you not understand? Look. The

Author made everything, right? You, me, Muffy, this garden, the world. And he is so wonderful that he never ever makes a mistake."

"Right, but ..." Jackson began.

"So if I am in charge of his perfect garden, then I need to *keep* it perfect." Burt sniffed and raised an eyebrow as she glanced at Jackson's shoes. "You've dropped a piece of lint. Pick it up, please."

Jackson looked down and picked up a piece of lint that had fallen from his shirt.

"Put it in your pocket for now," said Burt. "You can place it in the garbage receptacle on your way out. Don't worry," she continued. "With more hard work, you can be as perfect as I am."

Jackson burst out laughing. "Are you serious? You're not perfect! No one is!"

Muffy growled. Burt smiled sweetly, but her eyes had gone cold. "Yes I am." She flipped her ponytail. "And the Author loves me best."

"Excuse me?"

Burt twirled a lovely twirl, right in one spot, not disturbing a single flower. "He loves me best!" she sang out. "My clothes are neat and tidy, I speak nicely, and I keep his garden spotless." She stopped and stared at Jackson with a sudden inten- sity. "Now you ... You are a mess. Your san- dals are old and worn, there are some loose threads on your shorts, your toenails are too long, you have dirt on your knees, your shirt is ratty ..."

"I was cleaning the pool!" Jackson protested. Burt did not stop to listen.

"And I dig holes and plant seeds and weed the garden, but I still manage to stay clean and neat. Your hair needs cutting and your teeth are crooked. How could the Author possibly love someone as messy and sloppy as you?"

"Now wait a minute, he loves everyone!" Jackson began to breathe faster.

Burt rolled her eyes. "Of course he does. But he can't love everything the *same,* can he? That's like comparing his love for me with his love for a filthy rat that lives in a sewer. Doesn't make sense, does it?"

Jackson's heart began to beat faster. "But ... he loves people the same."

Burt smoothed her skirt. Her eyes peeked up at him from under long eyelashes. "You don't really believe that, do you?"

Jackson slowly shook his head. That couldn't be true.

Could it?

"You know," she said as she stepped toward him. "You can make him love you more."

Jackson was hyperventilating now. "How?"

"Well, for starters, how about you get cleaned up a bit?" Jackson nodded quickly. His brain was so fuddled and messy, like a tangle of knots.

Burt placed her little hand on his chest and slowly pushed him backward. "And I know how to make that happen. There's a beauty shop very close to here," she said, fluttering her eyelashes at him.

"But I'm not a girl!" Jackson protested. "I don't need makeup and a hairdo!"

Burt smiled. "Think of it as a transformation."

"Um ..."

Burt's little hand shoved Jackson hard in the chest and he stumbled and fell ...

... down a hole ...

. . . until he bounced into a gargantuan white hammock. (*Gargantuan* means huge, honkin' big.)

His fingers touched the fabric. Toilet paper.

"Yeeeeeees? May I heeeeeelp you?" a voice sang out.
It came from a chicken.

chapter

18

In Which Jackson Is Discussed

A little red bonnet with delicate lace framed the chicken's face. Her eye shadow was demure, her lashes just long enough, and her beak was a sparkly pink.

Jackson just stared.

The chicken ruffled her feathers daintily and puffed up her chest. "I aaaaaam Miss Pottle. And I can seeeee that you desperately neeeeeed my help!" She fanned out her wings and waved them gracefully in the air.

"Um ... I don't know if I should be here," said Jackson. "You see, I flew into this tree by accident and I'm trying to get home. So if you could just point out where ..."

"Girls! Girls!" the chicken interrupted. "We have compan-eeeeee!"

There was a skittering and scratching across the floor as ten chickens hurried to the hammock and lined up evenly.

Ten chickens stared at Jackson.

Jackson backed up, looking for a way to escape.

"He certainly needs work, doesn't heeeee?" one chicken whispered to another. She tittered and gave Jackson a look.

"No wonder he was sent to us," agreed the second chicken.

"Who could possibly love that?" asked another, not caring to whisper. Jackson felt his cheeks burning.

"Girls!" Miss Pottle admonished. (*Admonish* means to scold. Scolding is something chickens do a lot.) The chicken's feathers ruffled, puffing up, then flattened back down again, smoothing out.

"We have a boy in desperate neeeed of our expert-eeeeeese! Let's make him more lovable, shall weeeee?"

"If you could just direct me to the nearest exit . . ." Jackson spluttered.

"Nonsense! You want the Author to loooove you, don't youuuuuu?" Miss Pottle trilled. The other ten chickens clucked softly.

"Well, of course," Jackson said, "but I'm sure if you just point . . ."

"This is perfectly necessary-eeeee!" Her chicken eyes looked deep into Jackson's.

"Truuuuuust me . . ."

chapter 19

In Which Jackson Is Improved

In the flashiest of flashes, which actually felt longer, Jackson's hair was brushed, washed, snipped, dyed, and dried. His fingers had been soaked and rubbed, and fingernails clipped, filed, and buffed. His face had been washed, masked, toned, massaged, and moisturized. He was exhausted.

Very, very slowly, Jackson opened one eye. The ten chickens had all lined up, watching him with smug expressions.

Miss Pottle clucked a little cluck and smiled a beaky smile.

"Well now! Whoooo can't say you're not loveable nooooooow?" She bobbed her head and pulled Jackson over to the mirror.

Jackson looked into it.

And gasped.

chapter 20

In Which Jackson Is Absolutely, Positively Perfect

Jackson's fingers touched his face. His skin was glowing. His grayish-bluish-greenish-brownish eyes sparkled, and his teeth were so white! He had a new haircut and blond highlights. He wore a dark blue T-shirt tucked into clean hiking shorts and solid steel-toed boots.

Jackson laughed. He looked like a movie star!

Miss Pottle took his arm gently. "Now you're perfect," she whispered. "How could the Author not love you?"

Indeed. How could he not?

Which Is Full of Glee and Happiness

Jackson strutted out of the beauty shop. He couldn't stop touching his hair.

"Oh ho! Look at Mr. Fancy Pants!" a gruff voice called out.

Jackson turned. Stimple was tying up a garbage bag.

"Not bad, eh?" Jackson touched his hair again.

"You look . . ."

"Like a movie star?" Jackson interrupted, smiling even bigger.

"Humph. Yah, I guess you do." Stimple hoisted the garbage bag up to his shoulder.

"Thank you!" Jackson did a pirouette. (A *pirouette* is a twirl. It's fun for girls and boys of all ages!) But he looked a bit silly. So he pretended he was swatting a fly.

"All fancy-like."

Jackson's smile faltered. (*Faltered* means his feelings got hurt, and he's not as sure his new look is so wonderful, but he didn't want to show the gruff, large-nosed troll he's a little upset.) "Ah, you're just jealous, Stimple."

"If ya mean 'cause you're clean, well, I wouldn't mind a lavender bubble bath sometimes," Stimple growled. He hoisted the garbage bag onto his back with a grunt.

"Pardon me?"

"Nothing! Let's go."

"Are you taking me home now?" Jackson asked. He couldn't wait to show off.

But Stimple didn't answer. So Jackson followed him down a path.

chapter 22

A Very Strategic Chapter

They walked down the hall in silence, but Jackson's mind was going a mile a minute. How could he convince Stimple to help him get home? Maybe he needed a strategy. A sneaky plan. An opportunity. Jackson admired his fingernails for a moment, and then he had an idea.

"So, Stimple. How long have you been working here?" Jackson asked.

There was a long pause. "Humph. Feels like forever."

"How long is that?"

Stimple shrugged. "I was born here." They passed a few doorways but Jackson couldn't see anything down them. He just kept following Stimple.

"Really? That's so . . . interesting. How do you get born in a tree?"

Stimple shrugged non-chalantly. "I was born here and then I got a job. Blah blah blah." Stimple turned down a different hallway.

"What do you mean? Given a job as a baby? Where are your parents? Where's your family?" Jackson asked.

But Stimple ignored him. Because they had arrived at a door.

And not just any door.

chapter

23

In Which Stimple Is Most Unhelpful

The door was a bright cherry red with a black dragonfly knocker.

"I've got work to do. Wait in here." Stimple pointed at the door.

"But . . . wouldn't it be easier to just tell me how to leave? Just point the way out," Jackson pleaded.

Stimple shook his head. "Wait here."

"Or maybe you could just take me to Sir Shaw and he can take me home."

Stimple adjusted the garbage bag on his back, saying nothing.

"Look, I can help you collect garbage. Then you can get your work done faster and then you can take me home." Jackson reached out for the garbage bag.

The door opened.

In Which Jackson Is on His Own

Don't need no help," Stimple growled. And he turned and walked away.

"Stimple! Wait!" But Stimple had disappeared. Jackson looked down the hallway. Should he try following him? Should he try to find his own way out? Jackson looked through the doorway.

"Oh, great," Jackson muttered. But he straightened himself up, put a cheery smile on his face, and walked through the red door.

chapter

In Which You Might Experience a Bit of Déjà Vu (Which Means You've Totally Been Here Before)

He was in a garden.

The garden.

Jackson swallowed nervously. But then straightened himself. He totally fit in. He looked perfect. Burt had to accept him now.

As a light breeze tickled his arms, he wandered down the path, peeking around a large crab-apple tree, and found the sitting area, complete with its black wrought iron table and chairs.

He tiptoed toward the white gazebo, looking around for any sign of Burt. What was he nervous for? His armpits began to sweat. But there was no one to be seen, anywhere. Jackson tiptoed toward the chairs. He should be allowed to sit there now—he looked just as perfect as the garden. He put a hand on a chair, checking his shirt and shorts once more just to be sure. Why was he still so nervous? He felt like throwing up.

He took a big breath and pulled the chair out from the table and ...

Which, We Must Admit, Is Not Very Exciting at First

Nothing happened.

No alarms, no flashing lights, no net made out of industrial strength toilet paper dropping on top of him.

Jackson lowered himself into the chair, breathing a sigh of relief. He was accepted.

But as he breathed that sigh of relief he heard another sound. A deep rumbling—like thunder. It made the hairs on Jackson's neck stand up. He stood up and turned around.

There, twenty feet away, half-hidden in the pink rose bushes, was Muffy.

The dog's lips were pulled back into a snarl, show-ing off his white pointy teeth. A long string of drool swung in the breeze from his lower lip. His ears lay flat against his head. His neck fur was bristling like a thick mane of prickling quills.

Muffy lunged.

chapter

27

In Which We Hope that Jackson Is a Good Runner

Jackson turned and ran down the path, banging his knee against the wrought iron table in the process. Muffy's heavy treads followed close behind. Jackson ducked and dipped and dodged and hopped and leapt down the path, his heart pounding in his throat. He needed to hide!

And then, just ahead, Jackson saw it. A patch of sunflowers.

Jackson veered right, heading straight for them. He ran between the stalks for a ways, turned and ran left, and dropped to the ground. He held his breath.

Muffy ran past.

chapter

28

Which Is Not Particularly Long

Jackson had been very, very, very lucky. Everyone
knows you don't run from dogs. Usually dogs are
faster than you. Usually they will catch you. Jackson
knew Muffy would be back, sniffing out his trail. He
needed a plan. And not just any plan. A good one.

Jackson checked his pockets for something to throw
at the dog. Raw meat, a bone, a motorcycle. Nope,
nope, and nope. Nothing. He looked inside his satchel.
A water bottle, a roll of toilet paper, and a flashlight.
His fingers closed tightly on the flashlight. Would it
be heavy enough? He could hear Muffy's sniffling and
snuffling as he circled back, searching for Jackson.
Jackson stepped deeper into the field of sunflowers,
squeezing himself through the thick stalks. The sunflowers pressed together tightly but Jackson shoved
through, finding himself in a tiny clearing.

And there was a toilet.

In Which We Learn a Lesson about Unpredictability

Jackson almost laughed out loud. He covered his mouth just in time and let out a teeny, tiny snort instead.

The toilet was gold. The seat was gold, the base was gold, the lid was gold, and the tank was gold. The flush lever was a gold tassel swinging in the breeze. Jackson could hardly believe it. A gold toilet in the middle of a sunflower patch? Yes. That's just the way gold toilets are— unpredictable at best.

Jackson reached out to touch it, just to see if it was real.

There was a deep growl behind him.

chapter

30

In Which Jackson Has a Very Good Idea Indeed

Muffy's fangs were sharp and glistening with drool. His snarls were loud and deeper, and he had foamy froth all over his large black snout. Jackson slowly stepped behind the gold toilet. Muffy took one step forward. Jackson's clammy fingers clenched the flashlight tightly, waiting for the right moment. His breathing was uneven, and his skin was covered in goosebumps. He slowly raised the clenched flashlight overhead, waiting for the right moment.

But then he had an idea.

"M-Muffy? Are you thirsty?" Jackson cooed softly, lifting up the golden toilet seat.

Muffy's appearance changed immediately. His hackles dropped down, his ears perked up into two perfect triangles, and his teeth disappeared behind a goofy grin.

"Are you thirsty? Eh, buddy? Want a drink?" Muffy pushed forward and shoved his snout into the toilet bowl. Messy slurps and swallows echoed in the bowl.

Jackson heaved a sigh of relief. But then a horrible thought struck him: *What happens when he's done drinking?* Jackson searched his bag, trying not to make any sudden movements, and pulled out the roll of toilet paper. He tore off several lengths and began twisting them into a complicated braid. After just a moment he'd tied a makeshift collar.

Muffy lifted his head and stared at Jackson. That deep, low grumbling had started again. Jackson tugged the gold-tasseled flush handle and more water gushed into the toilet bowl. Muffy shoved his whole head back in, snorting and sneezing like a water buffalo. It was now or never.

Jackson's deft fingers slipped the collar around Muffy's neck and tied it, careful not to get the toilet paper wet, and tied the leash to the base. The slurping and slopping stopped. Muffy lifted his head and looked at Jackson, a big slobber of water splashing the ground and Jackson's feet. Muffy laid down, his head resting on his neatly-crossed legs. His big tongue lolled out the side, a glistening strand of drool hanging from it as he panted. And as Jackson watched, his eyelids began to grow heavy and droop. Muffy was asleep.

Jackson stepped back from the toilet bowl, quietly and stealthily slipping back into the patch of sunflowers before Muffy noticed.

Which Is Simply Full of Tears and Boogers

Jackson followed the path back toward the garden door. He'd go find Stimple or Sir Shaw—maybe Stimple would be done with his chores now, and would help Jackson find his way home! He looked around the garden, searching for the door.

A screech pierced the air. And then very loud crying and wailing. It was coming from the direction of the wrought iron table and chairs. Jackson rushed back to the gazebo, his heart pounding. The wailing grew louder with each step he took, punctuated by gulps and gasps and the honk of someone blowing her nose. He could hear the distinct sound of nose-blowing.

"Burt?"

chapter 32

In Which Burt Shrieks a Lot.
You'd Better Cover Your Ears.

A very messy head of hair was trembling as the body sobbed with loud sobs.

Jackson stepped closer, putting his hand on her shoulder. "Burt? Are you okay?"

The messy head of hair whipped around, and a very scowly face glared at Jackson. Burt pointed at the table and chairs. "Look at this!" she shrieked.

Jackson looked around. "What? What happened?"

"Someone *sat* here!" she hissed. Jackson coughed uncomfortably. "Um, well, I was going to sit down and then Muffy came and ..."

"You?" Burt stood up, her hands in fists at her side. "You sat in that ... *chair*?" Her voice went up a few decibels.

"Well, almost. I was clean and pressed, and I made sure not to touch anything else, but Muffy started chasing me so I bumped the table ..."

"*You bumped into the table?*" she screeched.

"It was an accident! See, Muffy was growling ..."

"You? You ... did ... this?" she spluttered, pointing at a glass lying broken beside a golden plate.

"Oh, I didn't realize. I'm so sorry, Burt. It really was an accident. Look, I'd be happy to ... let me clean it up for you." Jackson reached for the shards of broken glass.

"Don't touch anything!" Burt yelled. Her little hands shoved him in the chest with surprising force.

"Hey now! You don't have to shove me! I said I was sorry!"

Burt whirled on him, her face menacing with fury.

"You have ruined *everything!*" She took a step toward him. "I told you and told you! You were not supposed to touch anything!" Her face began to turn very red.

"Burt! We can clean ..."

"NO!" she screamed.

Silence.

Not a word, not a sound.

Jackson watched Burt's face change from red to pink. Her breathing slowed. Her eyes filled with tears.

"What do I do now?" she whispered. She looked back at the table and the broken glass. "He'll never forgive me ... and ... and I've worked so hard!" She gulped back a sob.

Jackson didn't say anything.

"Do you have any idea? Any idea ... how exhausting it is?" She turned and sat down heavily on a step. Her head hung between her knees, big drops of tears splashing the ground. Jackson sat down beside her.

"I worked so hard and ... I figured if ... I wanted so badly ..." Burt looked up at Jackson. "What do I do now?"

Jackson held out his hand. She stared at it, then put her little hand in his. "You don't have to do anything," he whispered. Her eyes grew big and she began to pull away, but he held on.

"Burt, the Author is like ... he's like a dad. See, last week I was practicing my baseball swing, and I hit the ball through a window. *Smash.* Just like that. I knew my dad was going to come out and yell at me, so I ran

88

and hid up in my tree house. I didn't come down for a long time. And then he came up to get me. I figured he was going to yell at me."

Burt nodded, fascinated. "He yelled at you, right? He kicked you out and now you have to live in this tree?"

Jackson burst out laughing. "No! I said I was very sorry and I cried and I asked him to forgive me and you know what he said?" Burt shook her head. "He said, 'That was a nice shot. Don't do it again.'"

Burt's eyes grew huge. "But that's your *dad*. That's not the Author. He won't forgive me. And," she said with a sniff, "he definitely won't forgive you."

"Burt, you're not getting it. The Author *is* like a dad. He loves you, and he always forgives you. He made you, right? Why do you think he made you?"

Burt blinked. "To serve him. That's my job."

Jackson laughed. "No! He made you because he wants to love you."

Burt shook her head so hard that her messy hair became a blur. "That doesn't make any sense."

"Sense or not, it's fact."

Burt squeezed Jackson's hand. "OK. That *sounds* easy. But I don't know."

"One step at a time." Jackson hugged her. "Now let me help you clean this up."

And they cleaned up. Jackson picked up the shards of glass and put them in the garbage receptacle. Burt swept the gazebo.

"Now what?" she asked.

Jackson smiled. "Now we have hot chocolate with extra whipped cream and chocolate sprinkles!"

chapter

33

In Which It's Time to Move Along

Jackson slurped the last of his hot chocolate and wiped his face on his sleeve. "So you really don't know how to get out of here?" he asked.

Burt dabbed at her mouth daintily with a napkin. "No. I've never had a reason to leave."

"But surely someone must know! I have to get home. I ..." Jackson paused. *Did* he have to get home? He thought about his circumstances. And he was still a little mad. And still not talking to his little brother.

"How about you just take me to the elevator and I'll figure it out?" Jackson said.

They both stood up and carried their finished mugs of hot chocolate with extra whipped cream and chocolate sprinkles to the sink (A sink in the garden? Yes. A sink in the garden.) and cleaned them out.

"Burt, do you know Stimple?" Jackson asked.

She frowned. "Yes. Grouchy fellow, isn't he?"

"I wonder why he's so grouchy."

Burt shrugged.

They had arrived at the elevator. Burt pushed the button.

"Well, thanks for everything, Burt." He held out his hand to her. She looked down. "Did you use an anti-bacterial wipe?"

Jackson sighed. "Well, anyway, see ya later."
And with a whir and a churn ...
DING!
The elevator door opened.

chapter

A Chapter of Grouchy Proportions

And where do ya think you're goin'?" came a growl from the corner.

Jackson jumped. "Oh, Stimple. Hi, Sir Shaw." Sir Shaw nodded. Jackson stepped into the elevator, and the door closed. Stimple scowled.

"Took ya long enough," muttered the tree troll.

"I was visiting Burt. Right where you left me," Jackson said.

"I suppose she gave you a hard time too?"

"No, actually, it all worked out in the end. She's really very sweet, you know.," Jackson said.

Stimple scowled even harder and mumbled something about "friends" and "la dee da."

With a whir and a churn and ...

DING!

The elevator door opened.

Yet Another Chapter

Bright greeny greenness was everywhere. Jackson
was so blinded by the greenness he thought he had
gone green-blind.

But he hadn't.

When the elevator door had opened, large green
leaves pushed their way into the elevator until there
was barely room to stand. Jackson held his arms over
his face. Sir Shaw just stood to the side, apparently
accustomed to this kind of bad behavior from leaves.

Stimple gave a low growl, and the leaves moved
out of the way. (Perhaps they didn't mind moving for
Stimple.)

Sir Shaw's white-gloved hand was on Jackson's
shoulder. Jackson turned to look at him.

"Find your adventure yet?" Sir Shaw asked.

Jackson looked at Stimple who was stomping down
a path. "I'm not sure. The garden was pretty cool,
though."

Sir Shaw's blue eyes twinkled. "Well, don't stay too
long. You still have that matter at home to deal with."

"How did you . . ." Jackson spluttered.

"Have a nice day, sir," he said, and gave Jackson a
gentle shove out of the elevator. And with a whir and a
churn, the door closed.

Which Ends on a Cliffhanger

How did Sir Shaw know? How could he possibly have known? Jackson scratched his head. Then he stamped his foot. How had he known what had happened that morning? Jackson shook his head. Sir Shaw knew nothing. Jackson probably just didn't hear right.

Jackson ran to catch up with Stimple.

"Where are we going now? Are you taking me home?" Jackson asked.

"I'll take ya home when I'm good and ready." Stimple whacked at a couple of dangling leaves.

"If you just tell me I can . . ." but Jackson stopped talking. And the reason Jackson stopped talking was because . . .

chapter 37

In Which Jackson's Eyes Just about Bug Out of His Head

Now I know you've seen some forts before. There are forts that you can make in your basement with blankets and boxes. And cookies. Only the best forts have cookies to eat. There are forts that you build yourself with broken bits of wood and some old nails from the garage. And while you nail the boards, sometimes you accidentally nail your fingers too. And then there are the forts you only see in magazines that someone has built out of mud and sticks.

But these forts were not like any forts Jackson had ever seen before.

There were forts with blue siding, forts with yellow siding, forts with cedar siding, and forts made of rough-sawn pine. There were forts with rope ladders,

forts with twig ladders, forts with fireman poles and slides, and forts with long zip lines going back and forth between them. Some were perched so high up in the trees that you had to climb a spiral staircase to reach them; some were half-hidden in the ground. Some of the forts had trap doors that required secret knocks to enter. Some had steep roofs that needed a long rope on a pulley to open. One fort had red geraniums planted in the window boxes.

Jackson could hardly contain his delight. He ran three steps toward the nearest fort when ...

"And wherrrrrre do you think *you're* gooooing, young man?"

chapter 38

In Which Stimple Comes to Jackson's Rescue (with Disastrous Results)

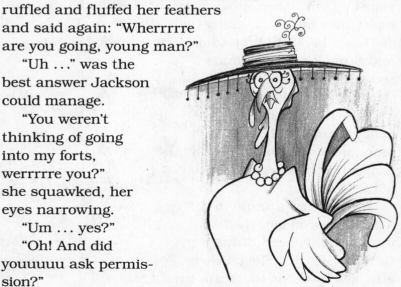

A rather large chicken was eyeing Jackson with disdain. The chicken was bright red, and on her chest laid a set of glistening white pearls. Her eye lids were slathered in blue eye shadow and her eyes kept twitching as though her long, false eyelashes were giving her grief. A bright purple hat (which was not at all becoming) was perched precariously on top of her head. She ruffled and fluffed her feathers and said again: "Wherrrrre are you going, young man?"

"Uh ..." was the best answer Jackson could manage.

"You weren't thinking of going into my forts, werrrrre you?" she squawked, her eyes narrowing.

"Um ... yes?"

"Oh! And did youuuuu ask permission?"

Jackson looked around for Stimple, but Stimple was nowhere to be found. Jackson cleared his throat. "Uh, no."

"And do you think it wise to go somewhere youuuu did not ask permission to go?" The chicken's eyelashes were twitching like mad.

"Well, I'm with Stimple, so I assumed that . . ."

"You *assuuuuuuumed*? And wherrrrre is Stimple now?" The chicken's eyelids seemed to be stuck together. She shook her head trying to free them.

Jackson looked around. "He was here a minute ago."

"So!" The chicken began to strut around him, waving her feathers wildly about. "Yooou thought you would just wander off on your own and you just *happened* to wander in heeeeere and you just thought you could help yourself, is that it?" Her orange beak was right up in his face now. She smelled of very cheap perfume.

"I . . ." Jackson backed up.

"Weeeeeell, I think that . . . BAAAWK!"

In the twitch of an eye (or maybe a few twitches if your eyelashes were stuck together) a white net fell on top of the chicken, pinning her to the ground.

"I say! BAAWK! Stop that!" She thrashed about, and Stimple's grimy hands scooped up the net with the chicken inside.

"Now listen here, Missy. I won't be havin' anymore of your nonsense! I'm the Keeper of the Tree and . . ."

The net flew around in a wide arc and smashed into Stimple's head. "Arggh! Ger off! Ger off!" The chicken attacked, pecking like mad. Bright red feathers flew out of the net as the chicken tried mightily to free herself.

"Stop! Stop!" yelled Jackson, struggling to be heard over the noise. Stimple paused for a moment, and in that moment the chicken pecked him hard on the nose. "Gaaaagh!" Stimple threw down the net and sat on it.

"You fiendish, heavy brrrrute! Get off of me! You're rrrrruining my hair!"

Stimple laughed. "Hair? Yer a chicken!"

Jackson ran over and started pushing Stimple, trying to get him off the net. "She didn't mean anything! She just wanted to know what I was doing!"

"Humph! Nosy thing. None of her business what we're doing here! I'm the Keeper of the Tree and ..."

"Oh, and you're doing a fiiiiine job letting this hoooooligan rrrrun around and smash everything!" the net squawked.

"I wasn't smashing anything!" Jackson protested.

"Well! I knooooow little boys, and I knooooow what you were intending! I was preventing the inevitable!" (*Inevitable* is something that is going to happen whether you like it or not. Like if you break your mother's favorite plate, going to Time Out is inevitable.)

"Want me to chuck her outta the tree?" Stimple laughed.

"NOOOOO! Don't you DAAAARE! I will repoooooort youuuuuu!" shrieked the net.

Jackson sighed. "Stimple, you'd better let her out."

Stimple growled, dark and low. He stood up slowly and opened the net. A very roughed-up and disheveled red chicken hopped out. Her feathers stood every which way, and the mascara ran down her face in angry black streaks. She fluffed and primped and straightened the purple hat on her head. "You've flattened my *corrrrrrdebos*!" she sniffed.

"What's a cordebos?" Jackson asked.

The chicken arched an eyebrow. "It is an austere
Spanish hat! And it's pro-
nounced *corrrrrrrdebos!*"

"I'm Jackson." Jackson
held out his hand.

She looked up scorn-
fully. "I do not knooooow
where that hand has
beeeen, thank you!
I am Miss Emiiiilia
Flaversham. You may call
me Miss Flaversham." Miss
Flaversham gave herself
a shake, then opened
her purse and pulled
out a compact. With a little white poof she wiped the
mascara from under her eyes, then pulled out a shiny
gold tube and reapplied orange lipstick to her beak.
Then, somewhere, she found another little poof and
some white powder. With quick, careful strokes, she
dabbed the poof into the powder and began smashing her face with it. White powder flew everywhere.
Jackson choked and began to laugh.

"And what are youuuuu laughing at, young man?"
Miss Flaversham did not look pleased.

Jackson gulped, trying desperately to stop the giggles.
His eyes were tearing up and he wiped them with his
sleeve. But he couldn't stop.

"N-nothing!" he gasped.

Miss Flaversham placed her wings on her hips and
gave him the hairy eyeball. (A *hairy eyeball* is a dirty
look, not an eyeball with hair on it.) "I demaaaaaaand
that you tell me what is so funny!"

"I, I . . ." Jackson looked at Stimple, hoping for help.
But Stimple was busy folding up the white net and
muttering to himself.

"I . . ."

"Tell meeeee! BAAWK!" she screeched.

Jackson pointed at her powder poof, still giggling. "My mom . . . my mom used that powder . . ."

"Yeeeees?" The chicken nodded, closing her eyes with a prideful smirk.

"She used that powder on . . . on . . ."

"Her face," Miss Flaversham finished.

"No!" Jackson gulped, trying to hold it together. "On my brother's . . . *ahem* . . . behind!" Jackson snorted, his entire body shaking with laughter.

"Weeeell!" Miss Flaversham sniffed indignantly and ruffled her feathers. Her mascara began to run again as her eyes grew weepy.

"Oh! No! Don't cry!" Jackson said. He tried to control his laughing. "I didn't mean to hurt your feelings!"

Miss Flaversham glared at him with her beady, blue-eye-shadowed eyes. Then she glared at Stimple, who was busy picking his nose. She sniffed and looked away.

"I forrrrrgive you, young man. You will find that I was properly raised and I do not beeear ill will toward anyone." A snort came from Stimple's direction. Jackson and Miss Flaversham looked over just in time to catch him digging through his beard. His thick fingers pulled out a half-eaten hot dog. He saw them watching, and popped the hot dog into his mouth. He chewed loudly, with his mouth wide open, until at last he swallowed.

"Listen lady, I've got work to do," Stimple announced.

"Why don't I come with you, and you can just show me the exit?" Jackson said.

"I beeeeeeg your pardon? Yooooou may call me Miss Flaversham. I'm no lady!"

"You can say that again!" Stimple growled. He pulled a full garbage bag out of a bin.

"That's not what I meant!" She ruffled her feathers again.

"See ya in a bit, kid." Then Stimple walked away.

"I am nooooot a babysitter!" Miss Flaversham hollered.

"Stimple! Wait! Take me with you!" Jackson yelled. But Stimple was already gone.

"Yoooou!" Miss Flaversham glared at Jackson. "Yoooou look like a troublemaker!"

Jackson sighed. But then had a very good idea indeed. "I'm sure you know this tree very well, Miss Flaversham."

She nodded elegantly, and Jackson continued. "I'm sure even you know the way out of this magnificent tree."

Miss Flaversham paused. Then she blushed as she wiggled her behind. "I can't really recall."

Jackson sighed. Was he ever going to get home? "Why don't you give me a tour, then? I'd love to see the forts."

"Fine."

chapter 39

In Which Jackson Misbehaves

You know when you're visiting someplace really interesting, like a science museum or a farm or a zoo, and they have such fascinating things that you feel you must absolutely touch something or you'll just die?

Jackson was in such a place.

Oh, the horrible temptation of it all! So many forts beckoning him, teasing him. How, oh *how*, could he convince Miss Flaversham to let him go inside just one?

The tour began.

"This fort is built like a barn. You can almost imaaaagine the animals inside!" she trilled, pointing with a slightly disheveled wing at a fort that looked just like a barn.

"Do you live there? Can we go in?" Jackson asked.

"Absoluuuuuutely not! I am nooooo filthy animal!" Miss Flaversham clucked.

They continued. "Theeeese forts are built like the one in *Swiss Family Robinson!*" she pointed with her feathers.

Jackson's fingers were getting twitchy. He was looking up at a set of three tree forts, arranged in a triangle. Between each was a swinging rope bridge, and each fort had a series of pulleys attached to various platforms that led up to the roof. Jackson itched to explore.

"Hey! Look out!" he yelled.

"BAAAWK! What? Where?" Miss Flaversham ducked, her wings protecting her purple-hatted head.

Jackson jumped up, grabbed the first rung of a rope ladder, and began to climb.

In Which an Argument Begins

Stoooop! Stop it! You come down right now, young man!" Miss Flaversham shrieked, her wings flapping furiously.

Jackson ignored her, climbing higher and higher up the rope ladder. Hand-over-hand and foot-over-foot he climbed until he reached the first platform. He pulled himself up and brushed off his shorts.

All he could see around him were branches and leaves and the very tip-tops of the other forts. Down below Miss Flaversham was pacing back and forth, bobbing her head, squawking away like . . . well, like a chicken.

"Yoooou are going to regret this!" she clucked.

Jackson ignored her and ducked inside the first fort.

It was cool and dark inside, and Jackson shivered a little. As his eyes adjusted to the gloom he could make out a trunk, a grandfather clock, and an old map that was hanging on the wall, showing some sort of island with forests and lagoons and a volcano in the middle. This, thought Jackson, would be a wonderful place to hide. He peered out the window to see if Miss Flaversham was following him.

Splat!

In Which Jackson Gets Egg on His Face

Jackson ducked back inside. His head felt gooey. "Aaaargh! I've been hit! I'm bleeding! I ..." He reached up to touch his head, then looked at his hand. It wasn't blood.

Splat!

Right in the face.

"Ow!" Jackson wiped his face. A thick yellow goop covered his fingers. He sniffed.

Egg?

He squatted down and peeked out the window. He didn't see anything.

Splat!

He ducked just in time to miss the third egg, and it smashed against the wall behind him, sliding goopily to the floor.

"You get down heeeere right now, you fiendish bru-uuute!" shrieked a squawky voice.

"Knock it off!" Jackson yelled.

"You terrible, bad boy!" Another egg hit the wall.

Jackson needed a plan. This was getting goopy.

Just outside of the side door was a small porch. Not a safe-looking porch, but at least it didn't have any gar-gantuan, hairy-backed spiders lurking in the corners waiting for their lunch. At least, none that he could see.

And then he saw his getaway.

A Tarzan rope.

chapter 42

In Which There Are Tigers.
Well, Just One Tiger.

Jackson wiped his eggy-hands on his
no-longer-clean shirt. He wiped his
face on his sleeve. He crouched like
a cat, waiting to pounce. He was
a tiger. A great and ferocious
tiger. A great and ferocious,
chicken-eating tiger.

Jump!

In Which Things Do Not Work Out as Planned

Jackson felt the wind rushing through his striped fur as he leapt. His long claws reached out as he grasped the rope, swinging through the air. He couldn't help the roar that burst from his chest.

"RoooooooAAAAAAAAARRR!"

He felt the wind, he felt the freedom, he felt the delight ...

He felt the tree hit him in the chest.

chapter 44

In Which Jackson's Day Just Gets Worse

Oooof!" Jackson groaned. Why hadn't he looked before he leapt? (If you're paying attention, you may find a moral lesson in this.) Jackson looked down and let go of the rope. He dropped onto the platform beneath him and lifted up his shirt to see a bright red mark on his chest. That would leave a bruise. He rubbed the tender spot and tried to hold back the tears that were welling up in his eyes.

And then, through the tears, Jackson saw the very last thing in the world he wanted to see. A pair of skinny orange chicken legs.

"Don't even think about rrrrrrunning!" Miss Flaversham said.

In Which Miss Flaversham Laments the Lack of Good Servants These Days

Jackson hid his face. Miss Flaversham's wing was held high, a fresh egg tight in her grasp. Her little pink purse was open, and Jackson could see that there were more eggs inside.

"Okay, okay! I'm sorry!"

Miss Flaversham paused, the egg still held aloft. "You surrrrrender then?"

"Yes," said Jackson in a very small voice.

"I did *not* give youuuuu permission to peek inside. I am in charge of these forts, and you will do exactly as I say!" she squawked.

Jackson nodded and stood up. He was covered in egg goo. Miss Flaversham handed him a bright orange handkerchief.

"What exactly do you do around here if you're in charge?" Jackson wiped his hair. Ick.

"I mind the tree forts," Miss Flaversham fussed with her pink purse.

"So you take care of them?" Jackson wiped his face.

"Whatever do you mean?" She slopped more orange lipstick on her beak. She missed and smeared a streak on her cheek instead.

"So you clean the windows and stuff?" Jackson scrubbed the inside of his ear.

"Certainly not! Filthy work. Men should clean windows, not well-bred chickens."

"Do you sweep the floors?"

"Of course not!"

"Do you mend roofs?"

"No. I cannot get up on the roofs. Are you implyyyyyying that I am a monkey?" She folded her wings across her chest and glared.

"You could use a ladder."

"Don't be ridiculous. I can't carry a ladder! Much toooo heavy."

"You could fly up." Jackson handed her back the eggy handkerchief.

"Chickens flying? Preposterous! Wouldn't think of it. Only fools fly around like twittering birds. I am not a silly twittering bird; I am a chicken!"

"Well, then . . . Do you clean the gardens?" Jackson asked, exasperated.

"No. All that dirt would get stuck under my nails." Jackson noticed that her long, scraggly claws were painted bright orange to match her lipstick.

"Well, what *do* you do?"

"You are not liiiiiiistening. I *mind* them. I make sure everything is in running order."

"Oh!" Jackson exclaimed. Miss Flaversham began walking down the wooden beams that led to the ground. Jackson followed. "So you tell the staff what to do?"

"No, no, no. No staff to speak of. Everyone is much too busy."

"Then you make plans for the forts. You figure out what would make them better. You would know if one needed a ladder fixed or had a hole in the roof."

"Oh, yes!" She bobbed her head. "I am very good at making lists."

"So then you give someone the list and ..."

"No! Of course not! They are myyyyy lists! Someone else would just steeeeeal them and pass them off as their own! Plagiarism is very ugly." (*Plagiarism* is when you take the cover off an *Alice in Wonderland* book and put your own cover on and pretend you wrote it.)

"So you spend all day making lists?" Jackson asked.

"Yes. All day," she said rather regally. (Well, as regally as a chicken can say anything.)

Jackson shrugged. "You're not much use then, are you?"

Miss Flaversham stopped walking and grabbed Jackson's arm with her wing. "I beg your pardon?" she clucked.

"Look," said Jackson. "My parents' job is to take care of us. To make money and make sure we're fed and clothed and loved. My job is to help out at home with the dishes and take care of my brother and sister. But you don't do anything here. You just make lists! How are you any help?" Jackson turned and kept walking. He really had to go home now. This conversation was getting annoying, and it didn't look like he was going to get to see the inside of any other forts. Why bother staying?

"Well!" Miss Flaversham looked wildly around, her eyelashes fluttering and sticking together. "I mind the tree forts!"

"You mean you just sit around and watch them all day. That's not a job," Jackson said. He was getting all sweaty and hot, and he still had remnants of egg goo on him. (*Remnants* are things that are left over, like the little bits of food dropped on the kitchen floor that your dog licks up.)

"I . . . I mind the stars!" Miss Flaversham blurted.

"What?"

"I mind the starrrrrs. They are mine!" she shrieked.

"No, they aren't. They don't belong to you." Jackson sighed. He just wanted a shower.

"Well then, who owns them?" *Cluck, cluck, cluck.*

"No one."

"Well, then I am the first to think of it! I mind the starrrs!" She gave a triumphant cluck.

"That's ridiculous." Jackson really, really wanted a shower.

"I do! They come out at night when I tell them to, and in the morning they hide when I tell them to."

"All right, then. Prove it," said Jackson.

"Proooove what?"

"Prove it. Tell them to come out. Right now."

"Rrrrright now?" asked Miss Flaversham, her eyelashes fluttering madly.

"Yah, right now." Jackson really, really wanted a shower. He'd even bathe in a puddle if there was one nearby.

"I don't feel like it!" said Miss Flaversham, and she turned away. "I'm not going to do something just because you told me to. Come back later when I'm not soooooo flustered. You bother me so." She began powdering her nose with the white powder that goes on babies' . . . *ahem* . . . behinds.

"Fine. Whatever," said Jackson. He looked around at all the forts, then back at Miss Flaversham. "Um . . . which way is the elevator?"

She eyed him suspiciously. "Why do you want to leeeeeave?"

"Because you won't let me look inside the forts, I'm covered in egg, and there's no point in me staying."

Miss Flaversham bobbed her head a moment, her eyes shifting back and forth quickly. Her brow furrowed in worry. "You don't have to leave immeeeeeedi-ately, do you?"

"I have to get home," said Jackson.

Miss Flaversham rubbed her wings together ner-vously. Jackson thought that she probably didn't get many visitors. "If you promiiiiise not to break any-thing," she blurted, "I'll let you go inside one fort."

Jackson raised an eyebrow. "Any fort?"

She shook her feathers uncomfortably. "Yeeees. Just one though."

Jackson's heart leapt. He could wait for a shower.

chapter 46

In Which Jackson Must Make a Decision

Which one, which one? Jackson wandered around the bottom of the branches, looking up into the forts, trying to decide.

There was a fort that looked like an old lady's house, with pink siding, white gingerbread trim, and lace curtains in the windows. (*Gingerbread trim* does not mean it's made of cookies. That sort of thing only happens in stories.) Jackson stood right under it and sniffed. Gingerbread cookies. Jackson shook his head and walked to the next one.

The next fort was a bright, shiny red with large brass fire bells hanging on the corners. Its black roof sloped into a high peak with a tiny window at the very top. Jackson listened carefully. He could hear fire truck sirens.

The next fort was made of sticks and coconut shells. It looked like something you'd find on a deserted island.

The next was shaped like a pirate ship. Its deep blue walls were studded with cannons, and a few tiny windows looked into cozy cabins. A mast rose out of the middle, soaring up into the branches. Tempting.

"I pick this one," Jackson said. And he began to climb the ladder.

chapter

47

Which Is Full of Possibility, but Ends on a Tragic Note

Jackson climbed quickly, hand over hand, gripping each rung of the rope ladder as the rough fibers scratched his hands. He climbed quickly, then swung a leg up onto the deck of the ship.

It looked like it had been a long time since anyone had been there. The wooden floor was strewn with fallen, crinkly, crunchy leaves. Jackson stepped through them, because on the the other side of the ship was a plank.

He jumped up to the base of the plank, envisioning pirates all around him, poking his back with their razor-sharp swords. He held his hand over his heart. "I die with honor!" he announced. But he didn't jump. There wasn't an ocean to jump into, and that ground looked pretty hard and pretty far away. Instead, he walked over to the cabin and opened the door.

Inside was a huge wooden ship's wheel. Jackson ran his hands over the smooth surface, gripped a spoke, and turned it to the left. "Arrr, matey! Off we go!" he cried. And immediately turned red. He wasn't sure if that was what a pirate was supposed to say or not. He didn't know much about boats and didn't want anyone else to know he didn't know much about boats. So he kept his pirate jargon in his head. (*Jargon* is the language you hear when two doctors are discussing cruciate ligaments and dilated cardiomyopathy.)

Jackson looked at the instruments and dials in front of him. He had no idea what any of them did. They were slightly dusty with cobwebs. He spun the wheel hard to the right.

And something fell on his head.

Which Contains a Mystery

Ouch!

Jackson rubbed his head tenderly. It still hurt from where Stimple had thwacked him. He looked to the ground and saw an old green bottle. He leaned down to pick it up. It was heavy, definitely glass, with a note inside. Oh, this was exciting! He turned the bottle this way and that to try and read the note.

Jackson tugged at the cork but it wouldn't open. He debated smashing the bottle on the wheel, but given it wasn't his fort and Miss Flaversham would probably have a heart attack, he decided that wasn't a good idea.

"Yourrrr time is up, young man!" a familiar voice squawked out.

Jackson sighed. He stashed the bottle in his bag and walked to the edge of the boat. Miss Flaversham was glaring up at him with her wings on her hips. Jackson climbed down.

chapter

49

In Which Jackson Learns the Importance of Conservation

"Dooooo come again and visit sooooon," Miss Flaversham clucked as she pushed him back toward the elevator with her surprisingly strong wings.

"Wait, wait! Are you taking me home?" Jackson dug his heels in a little.

"No, no, much too busy! BAAWK!"

"Well ... isn't there somewhere I can clean up? I'm all sticky from the eggs!"

Miss Flaversham clucked fussily. "Don't you have anything in your bag?"

Jackson rummaged in his bag, finally pulling out the bottle of water. "What if I dump this on my head?"

"No! Nooooo!" she shrieked, waving her wings wildly in protest. "Don't waste it! Just a drop!"

Jackson raised an eyebrow. He carefully unscrewed the top, cracking the seal. Miss Flaversham danced around him, fussing. "Just a drop, mind you! Don't waste a single drop!"

Jackson stared at the water bottle, then at Miss Flaversham, and then back at the bottle.

The chicken shook her head, her eyelashes sticking together again. "Just give me the bottle. I'll do it. You'll mess up everything!" Jackson handed her the bottle. Why argue with a hysterical chicken? No point, really.

Miss Flaversham took the bottle carefully in her wings and slowly raised it above Jackson's head. "Close your eyes now and whateverrrrr you do, don't open them!" she warned.

Jackson closed his eyes tightly and waited for the splash.

And waited.

And waited.

"Um, Miss Flaversham?"

"Shhhh!" she whispered screechily.

So Jackson waited.

And just then, a cool tingling began at the top of Jackson's head. It slid down his face, his ears, down his shirt and chest.

"Don't open your eyes!" Miss Flaversham shrieked.

The tingling trickled down his arms and legs and into his toes. He waited.

"All donnnne!" Miss Flaversham sang out.

Jackson opened his eyes. He was clean! All the egg goop was out of his shirt, his shorts, his hair! How was that even ...?

"All right, you're all clean, have a nice day!" said Miss Flaversham, and she shoved him toward the elevator.

"I guess I'll see you soon when ..."

"But not tooooo soon!" she sang, and gave him a harder shove.

Jackson stood in front of the elevator door. He turned to look back, but Miss Flaversham was already waddling away, muttering to herself.

With a whir and a churn ...
DING!
The elevator door opened.

chapter 50

In Which Stimple Is Extremely Grouchy

"Ya keep takin' off! I don't have all day to follow you around!" Stimple growled.

Jackson's eyes widened. "Are you serious? *You* dumped *me*! Again! With a big chicken! And she was grouchy—just like you! Oh ..." Jackson covered his mouth. Stimple had turned a deep shade of vermilion. "I mean ... oh, I didn't mean that. I meant ..."

Stimple grabbed Jackson's arm and dragged him into the elevator. Sir Shaw kept his gaze forward, not interfering. With a whir and a churn, the elevator door closed.

"I'm sorry. I just meant ... why won't you just take me home?" Jackson asked. "Wait. Is that a ... is that a *cob of corn* in your beard?"

"Why won't you just take me home!" Stimple imitated in a high, nasal voice. "Whiner." Stimple tucked the cob corn further into his beard.

"Hmph," said Jackson. Stimple stared straight ahead. The elevator went down. Jackson looked at Sir Shaw. Sir Shaw gave Jackson a look, a quick look, and then looked away. Jackson wasn't quite sure what the look meant. He racked his brain, trying to figure it out.

And with a whir and a churn ...

DING!

The elevator door opened.

chapter 51

Which Is the Fifty-First Chapter

Stimple shoved Jackson out.

"Hey! You don't need to be so rough!" Jackson shouted.

Stimple growled, but paused. "Humph." And he walked off down the path. Jackson paused, then chased him down and walked beside him quietly. He had to get Stimple to help him get home! How on earth was he going to convince him?

"So ..." Jackson began tentatively. "Nice day, isn't it?"

Stimple rolled his eyes. Jackson tried again.

"Do you have to collect *all* the garbage from the tree?"

Stimple sneezed. "Yah." He sniffed loudly and pulled a half-eaten roast beef on rye out of his beard. He threw it into his mouth.

Jackson and Stimple stopped in front of two garbage bags. "Want some help?" Jackson asked. Stimple just raised his eyebrows and kept chewing.

One of the garbage bags was a perfectly rounded, double-bagged, extra-strength, super-flex, pink-ribboned, freshly-scented bag. The other was a dirty brown bag with holes that were oozing blackish liquid and smelled like a festering burrito.

Jackson reached out for the perfectly rounded, double-bagged, extra-strength, super-flex, pink-ribboned,

freshly-scented bag. "I'll carry this one, if you don't mind."

Stimple shrugged. "Suit yerself." He hoisted the dirty brown bag and threw it on his back. Little bits of blackish liquid flew out of the hole, spraying the walls and Jackson's feet.

"Oh, *gross!*" Jackson muttered. He looked around for some fallen leaves to wipe it off. Oh, the stink was awful! He wished he had some antibacterial wipes now! He bent down to pick up his own garbage bag. Not too heavy. Must be Burt's garbage bag.

Jackson followed Stimple down the path. He had to stay about twenty feet behind, though, as Stimple's bag kept oozing out blackish liquid and festering burrito stink.

On and on they walked, the path seeming to lead nowhere. Jackson switched the garbage bag to his other side. The bag wasn't heavy, exactly, but his left hand was cramping up. Jackson hummed to himself.

After a few minutes he transferred the bag back again. "Stimple? Do we have much further?" Jackson asked. He was getting a little bored. And thirsty. And maybe a little tired.

"Oh ho! Gettin' tired, are ya? Thought you were a strong lad!" Stimple cast a glance over his shoulder.

"No, no. I'm just thirsty! Maybe we could stop for water? I think I have some on me." Jackson stopped walking and put down the garbage bag, reaching for his satchel to grab the bottle of water, and then happened to glance up at Stimple. A long, stringy strand of mozzarella cheese ran from his nose to his ear.

"Um ..." Jackson mimed wiping his mouth with his forearm. Then he opened his eyes really wide, staring intently at Stimple, and mimed wiping again.

Stimple had no idea what Jackson was doing.

"Stimple, you've got ... er ... What is that? Cheese stuck to your face? Is that ... where did you get french onion soup?"

Stimple brought his arm to his mouth and wiped. "Humph. Some friend you are," he growled.

"Wait, what? Are we friends?" Jackson asked.

"Not anymore!"

"What? Stimple!" Jackson dropped his garbage bag and threw up his hands. But Stimple just turned his back, pushing the leaky, smelly garbage bag into Jackson. Jackson heaved a very exasperated sigh. "Stimple," he said, "friends tell each other important things like if they have french onion soup cheese stuck to their face or toilet paper stuck to their shoes."

"Shoes? I got no shoes!" And Stimple began to trudge away.

"Stimple! I'm trying to help!" Jackson called out.

Stimple whirled around and stomped right up to Jackson, shoving his big nose into Jackson's face, his putrid breath smelling of onions and a very strong broth. Jackson held his breath.

"I don't want help from a lily-livered pipsqueak like you!" Stimple growled.

Jackson cringed. "You don't have to be nasty."

Stimple's hairy face grew purple. "An' you don't have to be such a whiner! You don't hear me complainin' about pickin' up garbage every day, do ya? I do my job, and I do it good! I was dumped by my own parents, and I've had to fend for myself every single day of my life! You don't hear me complainin', do ya? No! Because I'm tougher than you, and I'm stronger than you!" Bits

139

of saliva sprayed through the air as Stimple yelled. "I didn't ask ya to help me, did I? No! I don't need a needle-nosed tweedlehead followin' me around asking questions all the time! So quit followin' me!"

"I'm helping you because I'm trying to get home! If you would just tell me how to get out of this tree, we'd both be a lot happier!" Jackson shouted.

"Oh ho!" cried Stimple. "The truth comes out now! Yer just tryin' to get on my good side so I'll do what you want!"

"*I'm* selfish?" asked Jackson, incredulous. "Are you kidding me? *You're* the one who hasn't bothered to help me at all! You told me you had work to do and I had to wait. So I waited! Patiently! And now you won't help me? I'm helping you out of the goodness of my heart!"

"Oh, you are, are ya?" Stimple dropped the dirty brown garbage bag with holes that oozed blackish liquid and smelled like festering burritos. It made a satisfyingly squishy sound as it hit the ground. "Out of the goodness of yer heart?"

"Yes!" Jackson grabbed the smelly garbage bag.

"And not because you want me to just take ya home?"

"Well ... I'd help you even if you didn't take me home!" Jackson stuttered and spluttered.

"Oh, ya would, would ya?" Stimple shoved his nose into Jackson's face again.

"Yeah. I would!" Jackson growled back.

"Then ya won't mind if I don't take ya home!"

"What?" Jackson swallowed. And paused. "N-no."

"Ha! Ya right!" Stimple turned away.

Jackson took a deep breath. Something tickled his brain about the way Sir Shaw looked at him, but he couldn't quite put his finger on it. *Think, think, think.*

And the more Jackson thought about it, the more he understood that life was unfair. And the more he understood that Stimple had had it rough growing up. So a little piece of Jackson's heart hurt for Stimple. He felt bad for him. And that is called compassion.

"I'm sorry, Stimple," Jackson said, putting a hand on the troll's shoulder.

Stimple shrugged him off. "Got work to do. Leave me alone." Stimple grabbed the two garbage bags and walked away.

"Stimple!"

chapter 52

In Which Jackson Learns about His Roots

The elevator door opened, and Jackson went in. With a whir and a churn, the door closed.

"Good day, sir," said Sir Shaw in his dignified but polite voice.

"Hi."

"And how is your adventure going, sir? As expected?" Sir Shaw asked.

Jackson snorted. "Some adventure. I just want to go home, and Stimple . . . Stimple . . ." Jackson fell quiet.

Sir Shaw nodded knowingly. "Stimple is a rather complex character."

"Do you know him well?" Jackson asked.

Sir Shaw paused. "I know enough."

"Is that why . . . is that why you gave me that look?"

Sir Shaw chuckled, but didn't answer the question. Jackson looked to the floor, deep in thought. "Do you work here all by yourself?" he asked.

"Oh, yes." Sir Shaw replied. "Someone needs to man the elevator."

"But don't you get lonely?" Jackson asked.

"Sometimes." Sir Shaw's dark blue eyes looked into Jackson's.

"Doesn't anyone ever visit?"

"Not really." Sir Shaw pulled the gold lever, and the elevator lurched downward.

"Why?" Jackson was beginning to feel bad for Sir Shaw. He knew he'd feel awful if no one ever came to visit him.

"Oh, people used to visit. People used to visit all the time."

"What happened? Why doesn't anyone visit anymore?"

"The wind blows them away," Sir Shaw mused. "They get too busy and blow away. No roots, you see."

Jackson got a very puzzled look on his face. "I don't understand," he said.

"If you forget where you are from," said Sir Shaw, "if there is too much busyness in your life, you forget about what matters. You have no roots."

"Roots?" Jackson asked.

Sir Shaw smiled. "What is the most important thing in this world?"

Jackson thought for a moment. He really, really wanted to give the right answer. "Love," he said.

Sir Shaw nodded. "And who loves you more than anything else in the world?"

"My parents. The Author. My sister and ... my brother," Jackson admitted.

"And do you think anything would stop them from loving you?"

"Nothing!" Jackson's cheeks blushed red as he recalled a certain argument with his little brother over the scribbled journal.

"But what happens when you get really busy? Your family has a great deal going on. You do not end up spending much time together, right? You are busy getting things done."

"Yup. Sometimes it gets so busy we don't even have time to eat dinner together!" Jackson exclaimed.

"Now imagine you were busy all the time," said Sir Shaw. "And the family dinners stopped. And the busyness got even more busy. Then what would happen?"

Jackson thought for a moment. "Then we would forget how much fun it is to have dinner together because we'd get used to the busyness."

Sir Shaw nodded. "Exactly. And then you forget what is important. Your roots."

Jackson stared. "You mean, my family is my roots?"

Sir Shaw smiled. Jackson said nothing, his gaze at the floor while he pondered things. And then, with a whir and a churn ...

DING!

The elevator door opened.

chapter 53

In Which We Get to the Bottom of It All

"Y our floor, sir."
A long, dark tunnel, lit only by the dim light of flickering candles, stretched out before him. It was kinda creepy, kinda dark, and kinda scary.

"Um ... where are we?" Jackson asked. He cleared his throat, trying not to sound as nervous as he felt.

"In the elevator, sir."

"No, I mean—ahem!—which floor?"

"The bottom, sir."

"Why are we at the bottom? Is this the way home?" Jackson couldn't see anything down the hallway. Did he really have to go this way to go home? Couldn't there be a more cheerful, happier tunnel with lots of light and maybe a cotton candy machine to satisfy a sweet tooth?

"You need to finish your adventure, do you not? You cannot go home until you have finished what you have come to do." Sir Shaw raised a fluffy white eyebrow.

"But I never came to do anything! I got blown up into the tree by accident by some freak storm!" Jackson protested.

"Are you sure about that?"

"Am I sure about what?"

"That you are not meant to do something here? That maybe that 'freak storm,' as you put it, was maybe not an accident?" Sir Shaw peered into Jackson's face.

"I . . ." But Jackson had nothing to say.

"Things are seldom what they seem," Sir Shaw said.

Jackson looked back at the dark hallway. He took a deep breath.

"You can do it," Sir Shaw whispered. "Have some faith in yourself."

Jackson looked back at Sir Shaw and then nodded sharply. He stepped out of the elevator.

With a whir and a churn, the elevator door closed behind him.

chapter

54

In Which Jackson Hears an Ominous Sound (*Ominous* Means You'd Better Watch Out!)

It was hard to breathe in there. Jackson took deeper breaths, gasping a little as he coughed. The air was heavy, dank, and dark. The walls seemed to be made of dirt. Jackson reached out and scraped one with a finger. Spongy and moist. Dirt. Was he underground? Jackson reached into his satchel and pulled out the flashlight. He flicked on the switch and shone the light around. It didn't reveal a lot. It was still dark, the walls were still made of dirt, and it was still hard to breathe.

"*Tee hee hee!*"

Jackson spun. There was nothing there.

"*Tee hee hee!*"

His head whipped around, his flashlight pointing in all directions, trying to find the source of the noise. The tittering, laughing, giggling didn't sound friendly.

Jackson decided to be brave. He started walking. One foot in front of the other, his chest pounding as he gulped the stale air.

The tunnel seemed to get bigger up ahead. Jackson walked a bit faster. Then he blinked.

Which Is Not Particularly Long

The tunnel opened up into a massive chamber. There was a smell of something rotting in the air. Large black pipes ran every which way, climbing between each other, up and around and all over the room. And every few feet a brightly-colored rag was tied tight around a pipe.

Grunt! Grunt!

"Hello?" Jackson called out, just a little timidly. At least the giggling seemed to have stopped.

CLANG!

"Busy! Busy! Can't talk now!" *GRUNT!*

Jackson took a deep breath and decided again to be brave. He walked toward the voice.

In Which Jackson Knows a Thing
or Two about Knots

A short, squat, elfish-looking creature was tying a
purple rag onto a pipe. He was absolutely filthy. A
few scraggly strands of hair poked out from underneath a dirty hat. Jackson could just make out his
grimy pointed ears and the black, gooey smears all over
his uniform and thick fingers. The creature glanced at
Jackson, his bright green eyes like two bright lights in
the darkness, then went back to his work.

"I'm very busy. Please go away." He grunted again,
giving the rag one final yank.

Jackson watched him for a moment. "Do you want
some help?" he asked.

The elf's bright green eyes looked up in surprise,
but then he scowled. "You'll just get in the way. A lot
of work to do. Can't be bothered with all your chitchat
and whatnot."

"No, no. I'm great at tying knots. My dad taught me."

The elf gave one last tug on the rag, then stood up
and eyed Jackson up and down. "I suppose you can't
tie a clove hitch?"

"Of course I can!"

The elf reached into his dirty workbag and pulled
out a handful of colored rags. He looked Jackson over
again, then shoved the rags into his hands.

"Find a leak, tie it off."

"Are these all water pipes?" Jackson asked.

"Work!" yelled the impatient elf.

Jackson quickly shoved the rags into his own satchel and walked around, inspecting the pipes. He could hear dripping. He listened very carefully, following the sound to a large pipe that was already festooned with many bright rags. Liquid gathered at the bottom of the pipe, forming into droplets that made loud PLOPS as they hit the ground. The dirt was muddy underneath. Jackson reached up, swinging a red rag over the pipe and pulling it tight on the other side. His fingers moved slowly and carefully, pulling the ends of the rag through each other and then yanking them tight. The dripping stopped. Walking slowly between the pipes, Jackson listened for the next leak.

"I'm Jackson, by the way!" he called out.

GRUNT! "Alfonso!"

Jackson found another leak. He tied another rag. "What do these pipes hold?" he asked. "Water?"

Grunt. Snort. "Pipes ... they're *roots!*"

"Roots?" Jackson touched one of the pipes gingerly. It wasn't smooth like a pipe and it wasn't made out of metal or plastic. He squeezed it, and the dampness oozed between his fingers. He squeezed a bit harder, and a piece of bark came off in his hand. Oops. He patted it back on, looking around to make sure Alfonso hadn't noticed.

"Where did you think you were? A building? You're in a tree!" *GRUNT.*

"We're underground, then?"

Alfonso gave an unpleasant-sounding snort. "That's where roots grow," he said.

Jackson gave a final tug on a yellow rag and looked back at Alfonso. "Why are the roots leaking?"

"Because roots are porous. They have tiny holes in them to suck in or push out water. Don't you know anything about trees?"

Jackson *did* know quite a bit about trees, actually. He thought of several rude things to say to Alfonso but bit his tongue instead.

"But don't you want the roots to leak? You want to get the moisture everywhere so the tree doesn't dry out?"

Alfonso stopped mid-tug and looked at Jackson. He checked his watch. "How many did ya do?"

"Three."

"Humph. I'm keeping the roots from leaking because they need as much moisture as they can get. This here is one sick tree."

"What do you mean? Is it diseased?" Jackson squinted at the roots, looking for fungus.

Alfonso's dirty hands reached into his even dirtier work bag. He pulled out a sandwich and began to munch, paying no attention to the soil and muck getting all over his bread.

"Wumph. Mugletdd."

"Neglected? What do you mean?" (Jackson had a copy of *Thompson's Full Mouth Translation* and had read it several times, so he understood what Alfonso had said.)

Alfonso swallowed. "No one's taking care of it." He switched hands to eat. His sandwich, which had looked quite tasty, was now covered with dirt.

"What about Stimple? He takes care of the tree, doesn't he?" Jackson asked.

Alfonso snorted. Then started choking. Jackson smacked him on the back a few times. "Much obliged." The elf took another big bite. "Dapl whomey mah fes-ttsss." He swallowed a big swallow. "You know, only keeps out the riff raff."

"What about Sir Shaw?"

Alfonso stopped chewing. "Who?"

"Sir Shaw. The guy who runs the elevator."

"There's an elevator in here? When did that happen?" Alfonso wondered aloud.

Jackson looked at Alfonso strangely. "Just how long have you been working down here?"

Alfonso chewed thoughtfully, a piece of something awful stuck to his lower lip. "Hm. Ah. Ever since I was a young lad. Humph. Dunno."

"You don't know? How old were you when you started?"

Alfonso scratched his head. "Ah, let's see. Twenty? Yah, I was twenty. Just graduated from Rag-Tying School. Graduated first in my class!" His chest heaved proudly. He took another bite.

"And how old are you now?"

"Well, that I'm not sure of. I'm too busy to know what day it is!" With another grunt, Alfonso shoved the remainder of his sandwich back into his grubby satchel. "Back to work!" he cried.

"But don't you have a calendar or something?" Jackson protested.

"Work!" Alfonso yelled.

Jackson sighed and grabbed another rag from his pile. He found a leak near Alfonso and began tying a green rag on the root. "Don't you even have a calendar?" he asked again after a moment.

"Of course I do!" said Alfonso. "Everyone needs a calendar! Tells you what day it is and what time your dentist appointment is! It's at home, of course!"

"Where's your home?" A leak escaped from the rag and squirted Jackson in the eye. He tied the knot tighter.

"Huh. Well. I think it's around here somewhere." Alfonso shrugged, then walked off. Jackson tied off one last rag and followed him.

"You don't remember where you live?" Jackson tried to keep his voice friendly even though, truth be told, he wasn't sure he liked Alfonso very much.

"We-ell. It's been a while since I've been home. Terribly busy here trying to keep up with all the work."

"But what about your family?"

Alfonso's eyebrows furrowed in puzzlement. "Family?" He looked down and his forehead wrinkled. "I remember a wedding." His eyes lit up. "The bride wore white, the groom wore a tux, there were flowers everywhere, and people came to watch." Then he frowned again. "Was it my wedding or my brother's? Wait. Do I have a brother? Hmm." Alfonso shrugged and wiped egg salad off his mouth. "Ah, well. Back to work."

The elf grabbed another fistful of rags and moved among the pipes, listening for drips and tying them off when he found them. Jackson joined him, tying clove hitch after clove hitch wherever he heard the *plop!* of a leak. The damp air hung around him as he moved back and forth between the pipes, and after a few minutes Jackson felt himself panting.

"Why is it so hard to breathe down here?" he gasped.

Alfonso chuckled. "You're underground, boy. Not a lot of air here as it is. If the roots were growing properly, they'd aerate the soil and make it easier to breathe. But as it is, I'm trying to keep this tree from going anywhere."

Jackson stared. "Why would a tree go anywhere?"

"If you're gonna make me talk, you'd better help me work," he said. Jackson tied a magenta rag around a particularly leaky root. "Trees are like people," said Alfonso. "They need nourishment, water, air, sunlight. Wait, do people need sunlight?"

Jackson stared. "I guess so. I think a person would go a little crazy without seeing the sun for a while."

Alfonso looked at Jackson in surprise. "I guess it has been a while since I've seen the sun. Hasn't bothered me yet!" And he cackled in a very weird sort of way. "Anyway, this here is an old tree. A *very* old tree—some say older than Time itself. And it used to have great roots. Wasn't going anywhere. But over time trees, like folks, get itchy feet, you know?"

"Itchy feet?"

"Means they gotta move. Find something new, work somewhere else, do something new, be someone new."

"Why would anyone want to be someone new?" Jackson tugged on the ends of an orange rag and sealed off a very drippy leak.

"We-ell, imagine if you didn't like who you were," said Alfonso, grunting as he tied another rag. "You could just move somewhere new and pretend you're a whole new person. No one would know you, and you could be anyone you wanted."

Jackson stared at Alfonso. "Why would anyone want to do that?"

"Because ..."

"Because if you didn't like who you were, then that means you were doing things that weren't very nice. Instead of just taking off, you should apologize! Then you could work on fixing problems instead of ignoring them," Jackson burst out.

Alfonso stopped tying and peered at Jackson. "Wait. Wait a minute. What do you mean you can just apologize?"

"I mean just say you're sorry!"

"But what if what you did was really awful?" Alfonso began worrying his rag. (This doesn't mean he was worried about his rag or that his rag was worried. It means that he was twisting it about in a nervous way.)

"Then apologize!"

Alfonso nodded. "Yes, but what if it was really, really awful?" He worried the rag more.

"Apologize."

"Yes, yes, I see, but what if it was something really, really, really awful?" The rag had almost came apart in his hands.

Jackson threw his hands up. "Are you serious? A-pol-o-gize."

Alfonso paused. "But ... but what if ..."

"Alfonso."

"Yes, but ... you don't understand."

Jackson sighed. But then he reached out to Alfonso's shoulder and gave it a squeeze. "Just say you're sorry, okay?" Alfonso nodded.

There was a long moment of silence, during which Jackson pretended not to hear the sniffly sounds coming from Alfonso's direction. Instead, he looked around at all the roots and brightly-colored rags tied tightly around them.

"Are you sure this tree wants to leave? I mean, trees don't normally just walk away, do they? They normally just keep their roots in the ground and grow." Jackson wrapped a yellow rag under and over a root and brought the ends together.

"Well," Alfonso sniffed, "I don't know for *sure* that it wants to leave ..."

Jackson paused. "Then why are you doing this?"

"It's my job."

Both of them were quiet for a minute—then two— then three. Finally: "When was the last time you were home?" Jackson asked.

Alfonso looked at Jackson. "I don't know."

And then ... Wait. What was that noise?

chapter 57

Which Involves Neither a '66 Charger Nor a 371xp Husqvarna Chainsaw

Was it a '66 Charger?

Nope. Louder.

Was it a 371xp Husqvarna chainsaw?

No. Louder.

"What is that noise?" Jackson had to yell. "A '66 Charger? A 371xp Husqvarna chainsaw?"

Alfonso smiled.

"Squirrels."

chapter

58

In Which Our Hero May Be Headed for Disaster

Now you think you know about squirrels. Everyone knows about squirrels. Even people who live in remote villages far across the ocean know about squirrels.

And you don't think that squirrels are that loud. Oh sure, they're pretty annoying when they're screeching at five o'clock in the morning because the birdfeeder is empty. But you can usually turn on the radio, and you can't hear them anymore.

But have you ever been in a room completely *filled* with squirrels? I think not.

But that was exactly where Jackson was headed.

chapter 59

In Which Jackson Makes a Very Silly Decision

Jackson tiptoed down the hallway with Alfonso following closely behind. There was no need to tiptoe—the chattering drowned out any noise—but Jackson knew that squirrels scare easily.

A black door with gold hinges met them in the hallway.

Jackson put his ear up to the door. It sounded like there were about a million squirrels on the other side. He looked at Alfonso. Alfonso looked at Jackson.

Jackson reached out and grabbed the doorknob.

And turned it.

chapter

60

This Is Not Actually Chapter 60!
It Is Just Pretending!

Wouldn't it be just absolutely awful if I were to interrupt the story right here? I just want to point out that it's terribly late and you've been reading a lot already, and perhaps it's time to put the book down and go to bed, do your homework, feed the hippo, or mow the lawn.

But the next chapter is pretty fantastic, so maybe you should keep reading after all.

The *Real* Chapter 60

There were approximately 3,486 squirrels in the room. They had been all chattering at the same time, which is something squirrels normally do. They sat in a kind of circle, all facing one squirrel who was standing at a podium and chattering right along. It was like they were having a meeting.

And then all 3,486 squirrels stopped chattering, turned their heads, and looked directly at Jackson.

chapter

61

In Which Alfonso Is Not a Team Player

"Ah," Jackson mumbled.

The squirrels were staring at him.

"Alfonso?" Jackson whispered between his teeth.

"Just don't move. You'll startle them," Alfonso whispered back.

The squirrels were still staring at them.

"Why did you let me open this door?" Jackson hissed.

"I didn't know you were going to!"

The lights from the hallway reflected off 3,486 sets of eyes. Which means there were 6,972 black, shiny squirrel eyeballs looking at them.

Jackson suppressed a shiver.

The leader squirrel, in the center of their circle, dropped to all fours and began walking toward them.

"Quick. Do you have any food in your pockets?" Jackson muttered in Alfonso's direction.

Alfonso didn't say anything.

And the reason he didn't say anything was because the lead squirrel (whose name, incidentally, was Ralph) had stopped walking, risen up on his hind legs, and pushed his little black nose right up into Alfonso's face.

Alfonso didn't move. Ralph's whiskers quivered as he sniffed Alfonso, then he sat back on his haunches and stared. Jackson couldn't help but notice how large

Ralph was. Like the size of a dog. Not the kind of dog you carry around in your purse, but more like the size of a small Labrador.

"I-I don't mean any trouble, I'm sure.," Alfonso stammered.

Ralph tilted his head to the side. Then he pointed at Jackson.

"No, no. He was just curious, is all," Alfonso murmured.

Ralph turned, very slowly, to look at Jackson. Jackson swallowed and held out his hands. "I come in peace?" he said.

A strange garbling, chittering sound came from Ralph's mouth while his cheeks puffed in and out. The other 3,485 squirrels were still staring at them. Then Ralph let out another '*cheet!*' and they all lined up, rows upon rows of black squirrels.

A bead of sweat ran down Jackson's nose and onto his upper lip. "Alfonso?"

Alfonso whispered, "On the count of three, I want you to run as fast you can and get out of here."

"What?"

"One ..." said Alfonso and then promptly ran away.

Jackson didn't even think. He turned and ran after him.

If Jackson had taken two extra seconds to turn and slam the door shut behind him, the whole situation might have turned out very differently. But Jackson didn't take those two seconds, and before he knew it, 3,486 squirrels were close on his heels.

chapter 62

In Which Jackson Is on His Own
(Except for the Squirrels)

Jackson's heart pounded as he ran down the hall-
ways, desperately trying to follow Alfonso. But after
three turns, Alfonso had disappeared, and Jackson
found himself back at the main root system where
they had been tying rags. He ran to hide behind a
very large root.

Little footsteps skittered across the ground (that's
13,944 feet) and then stopped. Jackson waited, holding
his breath as best as he could. He peeked around the
corner.

A large semi-circle of squirrels all stood at attention,
their black, inquisitive eyes staring hard at Jackson.
Jackson had no idea what to do.

Ralph moved forward about ten steps and then
stopped. Jackson breathed hard. He had to do something, but what?

He looked around him frantically. Was there anything in his satchel that would help? He couldn't throw
a water bottle at them—that would only take out one
or two at best. He couldn't throw his flashlight—even
then he could only take out a few. And he didn't have
time to make a macramé net out of his toilet paper.
(*Macramé* is the art of tying knots to make horribly
tacky planters and wall-hangings.)

But then Jackson saw the bag that Alfonso had abandoned. He slowly reached out and grabbed the strap, sliding the bag toward him. He jammed his hand inside (which probably wasn't a good idea, as you never know what you're going to find if you jam your hand into something without looking to see what's in it first).

Jackson's hand hit something disgustingly gooey. He pulled his hand out and sniffed.

Peanut butter.

In Which Necessity Is the Mother of Invention

Jackson opened Alfonso's bag and pulled out a jumbo-sized jar of peanut butter.

No one moved. Well, none of the 3,486 squirrels moved. Actually, they moved a little bit. Their noses did, at least. Exactly 3,486 noses twitched ever so slightly at the smell. Ralph didn't say anything.

Jackson squatted and dragged his peanut buttery hand across the floor, making a peanut butter line. He knew the squirrels could smell it now. Their whiskers quivered ever so slightly. Jackson slowly stood up. He held up the jar of peanut butter over his head.

"Who wants to play a game?" Jackson shouted as loudly as he could. He tried to smile, but it is never easy to smile when you are terrified.

Ralph took a small step forward. The other 3,485 squirrels began shivering with excitement. Ralph chirped quietly and leaned in slightly toward Jackson, as if to listen.

"Yes, of course, everyone can play!" Jackson was just guessing what Ralph was saying. He hoped he was guessing correctly.   "It's called 'Hide and Seek,'" he said. "Anyone know how to play?"

Ralph gave a high bark, and all of the squirrels lifted their paws.

"I'm going to hide this jar of peanut butter," said Jackson. "But you all have to go inside the room, close the door, and count to one hundred. Then, when you're done counting, come look for the peanut butter. Whoever finds it wins the jar!" Jackson shook the jumbo-sized jar in his hand. All 3,486 faces looked up reverently at the peanut butter.

Ralph chittered and chirped. All at once, in unison, the squirrels dropped to their feet and ran back the way they had come. Jackson followed them, the jar still in his hands. "Don't forget to count to one hundred!" he yelled. "And no cheating!" He closed the black door and pulled out the toilet paper.

With a series of complicated knots and about thirty seconds later, Jackson had rigged a net to fall onto whoever opened the door. He put his ear to the door and listened. He could hear loud barking and chirping. Jackson laughed. He knew squirrels couldn't count. They might be there for a while.

At least, he didn't think they could count.

He ran down the hallway toward the root room and began digging a hole with his bare hands to bury the peanut butter.

"Want some help?"

chapter 64

In Which the Squirrels Learn to Count to One Hundred

Jackson looked up to meet a pair of bright green eyes. "Why did you take off? That was a really mean thing to do!" Jackson hissed as he dug faster.

Alfonso began digging as well. "What do you mean? I said to run ..."

"On the count of three!" Jackson finished for him. "That wasn't three!"

"It wasn't? Huh." Alfonso kept digging. "So, what are we doing?"

"We're burying the peanut butter, and then I'm out of here!"

"Why are you burying my lunch? I like peanut butter!" Alfonso complained.

"Um, I'm saving my life. And probably yours. Quit complaining and help me!" Jackson threw the jar into the shallow hole and scrambled to cover it back up. They patted the soil down and threw some rags on top to disguise the hole.

"Let's get out of here! Follow me!" Alfonso stood up and began running. Jackson jumped up and followed closely behind.

A low rumble vibrated the ground.

"I think they figured out how to count to one hundred," Jackson said.

"Or they're cheating. They *are* squirrels," Alfonso said, hardly pausing for a breath as they sprinted down a hall.

The rumbling was getting louder.

"Quick. Duck in here!" Jackson called out to Alfonso.

They climbed into a hole in the wall, shimmied through a very tight tunnel, and finally found themselves in a much larger room.

"Wait. Wait!" Alfonso called out. Jackson stopped and looked back at him.

"I know this place!" Alfonso began to walk around the room, his eyes wide as he touched the walls.

Jackson looked around the room.

It looked like the inside of a house.

A round table with four wooden chairs sat in the middle of the room. There were two place settings and a vase with dried dusty flowers off to the side.

Jackson followed Alfonso around the room. Little shelves filled with books, knickknacks, troll dolls with crazy hair, and framed pictures, lined the walls. Jackson picked up one of the pictures and studied it. A short, squat elf was smiling as he held a short female elf beside him. Jackson brought the picture to Alfonso. "Is this you?" he said.

Alfonso trembled as he reached out to take it. "Zuzu," he breathed.

"What?"

Alfonso traced the image of the female elf. "Zuzu. That's ... that's my wife." He hugged the frame.

"Where is she now?" Jackson asked.

Alfonso looked at Jackson blankly. "I—I don't know!" Alfonso ran to the next room. Jackson followed.

A large bed, neatly made with an old quilt was against the wall. And lying on the bed was a very small, very old elf with long, dirty red hair. She wasn't moving.

Alfonso began to scream.

chapter 65

In Which We Witness a Joyful Reunion

Sometimes sad things happen. Some things you didn't think would happen *do* happen. Especially when you least want them to.

But this is not one of those times.

Zuzu's eyes opened. And she screamed.

Alfonso jumped back and Jackson jumped back and then Zuzu jumped up.

Zuzu reached out for Alfonso. "Are you a—a dream?" she asked.

Alfonso began to tremble. Then he ran forward and embraced her.

Jackson smiled and turned away, because sometimes people need a moment of privacy. Jackson knew that this was one of those times. Jackson went back into the main room and sat down at the table. And waited.

But the rumbling was getting louder.

And closer.

chapter 66

Which Is Only Six Sentences Long

Um, guys?" Jackson called to the other room. "I'm glad you've found each other, but ... they're coming."

Zuzu appeared in the doorway. She looked up at Jackson with her bright brown eyes. A look of fierce determination came over her face.

"Let them come," she said.

Which Is a Little Bit Longer than the Last Chapter

Zuzu reached into the closet and pulled out a large jar of peanut butter. Jackson frowned. He peeked into the closet. There must have been hundreds of jars of peanut butter there, all stacked up.

Zuzu walked to the front door and waited. Alfonso grabbed a jar of peanut butter as well and gave one to Jackson. "I always knew that peanut butter was important, but I couldn't remember why," Alfonso said. "But I always carried a jar around." Zuzu smiled and squeezed his arm.

The rumbling got louder. And there was a definite ... squeaking noise. Yes, a very loud squeaking. Actually, it sounded like many squeakings.

"When I give the word," said Zuzu, "we open the door and ..."

BOOM!

BOOM!

BOOM!

"Now!" cried Zuzu. Alfonso took a deep breath and flung open the door.

"Yes? May I help you?"

In Which Alfonso Finds a New Line of Work

A very large ball of white toilet paper netting, black
fur, and sticky peanut butter stood before them.
Each of the 3,486 squirrels was squeaking indignantly.
Ralph pulled himself through a mess of squirrels to
the front of the crazy net. He chirped unhappily.

"Ah, ah, I see!" said Alfonso.

"What he's saying?" Jackson asked. He held his jar
of peanut butter behind his back.

"Shhh!" Zuzu hissed.

"Yes, I'm sure you're uncomfortable," Alfonso was
saying, "but that's all part of the game." Ralph waved
his paws around and the other squirrels kept on chattering.

"Of *course*, I'll help you out. You do understand
that the net was all part of the game? No? Ah. That's
how humans play, you see. No harm, no foul." Alfonso
reached out and snipped apart the toilet paper net.
Slowly but stickily, 3,486 squirrels disentangled themselves from the mess. They all lined up behind Ralph.

"So, who was the one to find the peanut butter?"
Jackson asked. He was feeling a bit braver now.

Ralph squeaked and barked. Alfonso nodded.

"Er ... slight mishap. Better let them all win,"
Alfonso whispered.

Jackson looked down uncertainly. "Are three jars of peanut butter enough?" he asked.

Zuzu nodded firmly. "I only give out one jar a month."

Jackson held out his jar, then Ralph and Zuzu handed over the other two jars. "Thank you for playing! We'll do it again soon!" Ralph chirped, and all 3,485 squirrels followed him as he left.

Zuzu shut the door and leaned back against it. "All right, what just happened?" Jackson asked. And then he saw that Alfonso and Zuzu were clutching their bellies and laughing until the tears streamed down their cheeks.

"We tricked them again!" cried Alfonso. "Squirrels are not the brightest creatures, are they?"

Zuzu giggled. She grabbed Alfonso's hand and pulled him into the kitchen. "Tell me what happened to you! Where did you go? Where have you been? I thought you were dead!"

Alfonso sat down on one of the kitchen chairs and pulled Zuzu down onto his lap. "I'm not letting go of you anymore!" he laughed.

And they had a long discussion. A discussion which would take far too many pages to include and would be too daunting to read. (*Daunting* means discouraging, like when you're faced with a bloodthirsty dragon and all you have to defend yourself with is a spoon.) Alfonso told Zuzu how he enjoyed his job so much that he would forget to come home. Soon he forgot who he was and where he was from, until Jackson helped him find his way home. Zuzu told Alfonso how she had tried looking for him a few times, but she was too afraid of the squirrels to venture far from the house. And so she had stayed at home to cook and clean and wait. And, of course, she gave the squirrels a jar of peanut butter every month so they would leave her alone while she went out to get groceries and garden.

"So now what, Alfonso?" Jackson asked.

"Well, I definitely need a new job. Maybe something that doesn't involve rag-tying?" Alfonso laughed.

"Are you any good at repairing other things?" Jackson asked.

"Oh, he's the best!" Zuzu cried, squeezing her husband's hand.

"You know . . . I met a chicken, er . . . Miss Flaversham. She might need help maintaining and repairing forts. But she's not underground. She lives up in the branches. Would you mind moving?"

Zuzu's eyes danced with delight. "Really, truly? We can move out of this hole and live in the sky!"

"I'm never letting you go, ever again!" Alfonso said to her. Zuzu kissed his nose.

"By the way," said Jackson, "do you guys know how to get out of here?"

"Get out of where? The tree?" Alfonso shrugged. "I haven't been anywhere."

Zuzu shook her head. "No idea."

Jackson nodded. He'd find his own way out. Somehow.

In Which There Is No Room
in the Elevator

Jackson wasn't sure how Alfonso and Zuzu managed to get everything packed so quickly. But they were definitely determined to move out, and Jackson was able to lead them back to the elevator without too much trouble. Well, maybe a little. He got lost twice and once had to disentangle them from a rather large spider web, but all in all they made it without too much trouble.

Jackson pushed the call button on the elevator door.

"Ooh, I'm so excited!" Zuzu cried. She patted her red hair (it was perfect, Alfonso told her), and tears sprang to her brown eyes.

With a whir and a churn ...

DING!

The elevator door opened.

Jackson grinned. "Hi, Sir Shaw! This is Alfonso and Zuzu. Alfonso wants to go work with Miss Flaversham. Do you think that's okay?"

Sir Shaw looked Alfonso up and down. Then he smiled a little smile. "A change of job when the time is right is always welcome. I'm sure there will be no problem." Zuzu clapped her hands and Alfonso beamed, his bright green eyes shimmering like stars.

They all squeezed into the elevator. Uncomfortably. With a whir and a churn, the elevator door closed.

"Urr ... can you get your elbow out of my back?" Jackson asked.

Alfonso grunted. "Not enough room in here!"

"Sir Shaw? Why don't you stop the elevator and I'll get out?" Jackson asked. "You can come back for me later."

"A splendid idea, sir," Sir Shaw murmured.

As the elevator door opened, Jackson fell out. Literally. He hit the ground and landed on his stomach. *Oof.*

"Good-bye, Jackson! We'll never forget your kindness!" Zuzu called out.

"Yeah, thanks a lot, we really ..."

And with a whir and a churn, the elevator door closed.

In Which Jackson Gets
Sick of Waiting

Jackson looked up. It certainly wasn't very bright in the room. *Was* it a room? He stood up to see more clearly. And then he stepped back, his heart lodged firmly in his throat. Because just six inches beyond his feet, the floor came to an abrupt end.

Jackson was standing on the edge of a precipice. (A *precipice* is that exact spot where you lose your breath when looking over the edge of a cliff.) If he squinted and peered across the canyon before him, he could see something that might be a dead branch, but the far side was about thirty feet away.

Jackson shrugged. Sir Shaw would be back soon.

He sat down and waited.

And waited.

And waited.

Jackson sighed and looked for the elevator button to push, but there wasn't one. His fingers searched the engraved door, looking for a secret button or lever. He searched the sides, thinking maybe this was a fancy floor, and it would have some sort of unusual button. But in a room with a huge gully in the floor? Jackson looked around, pushing aside the dusty cobwebs that covered the sides of the elevator door. There were no leaves here. He thought he must still be underground.

Jackson felt his muscles tighten as he fought the panic rising in his chest.

He banged on the door with his fists.

"Sir Shaw! Sir Shaw!" he yelled, trying to keep the fear out of his voice.

He tried squeezing his fingers between the edge of  the door and the wall to pry it open, but it was stuck tightly. Jackson reached into his bag and grabbed his flashlight. He banged it on the door, but it didn't make much noise at all.

"Sir Shaw! Stimple? Burt? Anyone! I'm stuck!" Jackson yelled. And he yelled again. And again. But there was only silence.

Jackson walked to the edge of the canyon.

"Oh dear," Jackson whispered. How was he supposed to cross that?

In Which, It Must Be Admitted, Jackson Cries

Jackson slowly crawled toward the canyon. He inched toward the edge.

The canyon looked like it had been made by something very heavy crashing through the floor. The edges were rough and stubbly, with little sharp bits sticking straight out. Jackson took a deep breath and looked down. Darkness. Jackson shone his flashlight beam into the canyon.

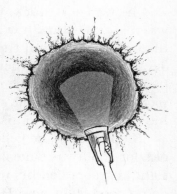

Darkness.

A black, dark, void emptiness.

Jackson slunk back to the door. He thought it must be getting late. He checked his watch, squinting to get a better look in the dim light. But the hands weren't moving. He shook the watch and held it to his ear. Either time meant nothing here or the battery had died.

Jackson brought his knees to his chest and breathed. He took out his water bottle and had a sip. He was very thirsty. But he didn't want to finish it. What if ... Jackson didn't want to think it, but he thought it anyway ... what if he was stuck here? Surely

Sir Shaw would remember to return for him, wouldn't he? Jackson hugged his knees tightly.

He heard a scurrying in the darkness below and shuddered. He flicked on his flashlight, and aimed it down into the hole. Nothing. Jackson leaned over a bit farther, straining to see, and, almost without realizing it, he kicked out his left leg to adjust his balance. And he heard, all of a sudden, the very worst sound in the world. The *glugluglug* of water escaping from a bottle.

Jackson spun around to see a puddle growing behind him. He grabbed the water bottle and tilted it upright, but he could tell by the weight that it was almost empty. Jackson smacked his forehead. Stupid! Stupid! Stupid! Tears formed in his eyes. Why hadn't he put the cap back on? There was little now to drink, and he was still stuck, with nowhere to go and no idea when—or if—Sir Shaw was coming back. He checked his watch again, but the hands still weren't moving. Jackson heaved another sigh then lay down on his back and stared at the ceiling. He would not cry. He *would not cry.* But tears still fell from his eyes, down his cheeks, and into his ears.

"Stop crying!" he yelled. He was ten and a half years old, for goodness sakes! Jackson scrunched his eyes tight and steadied his uneven breathing. Crying would do no good right now. He cleared his throat a few times because that is an excellent way to stop crying. You should try it sometime. Although it doesn't work very well if you are terribly sad. In this case, it did not work.

Jackson had a good cry. No, that doesn't sound right. Jackson had a very sad cry.

So Jackson lay there, swallowing and clearing his throat, his poor mouth parched and raw from thirst and from yelling. Jackson made himself sit up. He surveyed the area again. Maybe there was a way out, and he just hadn't found it yet.

He looked up for ladders, swinging vines, or trap doors. He looked across the canyon to the other side. It was still very far away.

Jackson lay down again. He rolled over onto his stomach, resting his chin on his folded arms, and began to hum.

There *had* to be a way out. He just needed to look harder. He went through the options again.

No vines to swing across on? Check.

No ladders to climb? Check.

No buttons to summon the elevator? Check.

Jackson looked at the ground a few feet away from his face.

Something glistened.

Jackson unfolded his arms and stretched out his fingers, hesitant at first, and then touched the glistening. It was wet. He smelled his fingers. It didn't smell like anything. He carefully licked his fingers. It didn't taste like anything. Water? He sat up, shined his flashlight, and found a stream of water running toward the canyon edge. It must be the water that had leaked out of his bottle! Jackson bent down and began slurping. He didn't let himself think about the dirt or dust or spider webs or bits of wood particles that he could be ingesting.

On his hands and knees he crawled, following the stream, slurping it up. He had to stop twice to remove woodchips from his teeth, but it was still satisfying. He came to the very edge of the broken floor. And blinked in disbelief.

In Which Water Behaves Very Oddly (Part I)

The water continued on, past the broken edge, and hung in mid-air.

Jackson rubbed his eyes. And blinked. And coughed for good measure. Was this even possible?

His fingers stretched out, and he felt the craggy rocks on the edge of the floor, the sharp splintered ends. But his fingers went right through the puddle at the end of the stream.

Jackson just sat there. Water that just hung in the air?

And then Jackson got an idea.

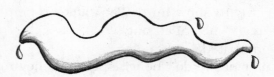

He pulled the toilet paper out of his bag, ripped off a piece, and crumpled it into a ball. He aimed and threw it into the canyon. And down it fell, disappearing into the blackness.

So why was the water not falling?

Something nagged at Jackson's mind. Pulled at it, distracting his thinking. He thought about Stimple. He thought about the troll's hideous nose hair, about his grouchiness and complacency. He thought about . . .

Wait. What if all of this was about faith?

But faith in what? Faith that he wouldn't fall? Faith that someone would come looking for him? Faith that he would make it home? What to do, what to do?

"What do I do?" Jackson called out to no one in particular. And no one answered but his own voice, echoing from across the chamber.

"Tell me what to do," Jackson whispered softly.

A hazy image formed briefly, hovering above the precipice, and then disappeared.

Jackson focused his eyes on that spot. "Tell me what to do!" he yelled. Nothing.

He frowned.

This was obviously something the Author had created. The Author wouldn't leave him here to figure everything out all by himself, would he? What was the Author trying to show him? Was Jackson being tested? "Is this a test?" he called out.

Jackson waited.

"Tell me what to do," he whispered, believing with all his heart that something would happen. And the hazy image appeared again, briefly.

Jackson knew what to do.

In Which Jackson Looks Down

Jackson grabbed the roll of toilet paper and unraveled it. He pulled the end through the belt of his shorts and tied a clove hitch.

This is how you tie a clove hitch in case you ever need to tie toilet paper to yourself. Or tie up your dog because he's not allowed into the ice cream store with you.

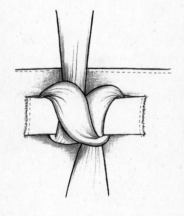

Then Jackson took what was left of the roll and shoved it in between a few broken roots. He shouldered his bag, tightened the strap, put the flashlight back inside, and walked resolutely to the edge of the canyon. The Author had always kept him safe. Many, many times before.

Jackson was planning not to look down, but of course he did and of course it was a mistake. The dark abyss looked even darker and deeper than before. Jackson swallowed. And then he began to tremble and shake.

Face your fears, he thought to himself.

And he took a step.

chapter

74

In Which Nothing Bad Happens

I want to tell you right now that nothing bad happens. I wouldn't want you to worry or anything, so I just thought I'd interrupt and tell you that everything will be fine.

Nothing bad happens.

Oh, except that Jackson fell.

In Which Something Awful Is Lurking

Jackson didn't even yell. He was too surprised. He fell and fell and fell and then, with a sharp jerk, he stopped. He hung sideways as the toilet paper held his shorts and him within them. He squiggled and wriggled and looked around. Darkness.

Jackson was glad the strap had been across his chest, or the bag would have fallen off. He reached into his bag and pulled out his flashlight. He flicked it on and pointed straight down. He could see the bottom now, but it was still just a little too far to drop. Jackson shone his light on the  side of the canyon in front of him. Nothing to grab. He shone the light down the wall beside him. Something was there! Something was moving!

Oh my goodness ... was that ... a rat?

Which Is Too Terrifying to Even Have a Title

This part coming up is a little bit scary. Just a bit. If it's nighttime, you should stop reading right here and go to sleep so you won't have bad dreams. (Your dreams should be about ponies and candy and bubblegum and winning the Super Bowl.) If it's daytime and you aren't prone to day-mares, then by all means, keep reading.

"Hello?" Jackson called out.

The huge rat turned slowly, its long pink tail swishing the dirt across the ground. His dirty pink nose and long whiskers quivered, and a chill went through Jackson's bones as he realized that the rat was smiling, leering at him with scraggly front teeth. (*Leering* is a creepy smile that someone gives when they are really mean and nasty inside.)

"Why, hello," the rat smiled. His voice sounded like nails scraping down a chalkboard. "Stuck, are we?"

"Um, no. Not quite. Just had a little tumble," Jackson said. He shivered.

"Didn't break anything or hurt ourselves, did we?" The rat stepped closer. Jackson noticed that the rat was standing on a ledge that jutted out from the side of the canyon. Beside him was a tunnel.

Jackson swallowed. "No, no, I'm fine!" he called out cheerfully.

The rat tilted his head slyly. "We don't look fine. In fact"—the rat stepped closer, his nose sniffing at Jackson—"we look quite ... trapped."

"Oh! Ho! No, no! I'm just practicing my rock-climbing abilities. And my knot-tying skills. I know quite a bit about knots, you see." Jackson wriggled so he could face the rat.

"Perhaps ... perhaps we need assistance?" The rat smiled. "Be more than happy to help us out."

"No, thanks! I'm good! Just gonna have a little rest and then climb right back up!"

"Perhaps ... we're thirsty? Need some tea? Tea is very delicious for us. Why not climb down and have some?"

"Thank you, but no. My friend is waiting for me up top. He'd be very concerned if I didn't get back soon." Jackson thought fast. "Which reminds me, I should probably let him know I'm okay."

The rat watched Jackson steadily.

"I'll start climbing in just a minute! All good here!" Jackson yelled to the top of the cliff. But he knew no one was listening.

The rat took another step forward. He was only ten feet away now. Jackson could smell festering garbage coming from the rat's direction. It smelled like rotten bananas and burnt hair and decaying meat. Jackson tried to hide his distaste, but the rat saw him wrinkle his nose.

"Don't like the way we smell? Well, when you live in garbage, you feast on garbage, and you become gar-bage." He swished his pink tail again.

"No, no! I just have to sneeze," Jackson explained.

The rat sat down. "We'll just watch the climb, won't we?"

"Uh, no, no. You go ahead. I'm sure you have lots to do."

The rat smiled again. "Not in a hurry at all. Besides," he licked his teeth, "we might need assistance. Wouldn't want to fall and hurt ourselves. Might get ..." he snickered evilly, "might get ... really hurt. Poor babies."

Oh dear. Jackson looked up to the top of the cliff. It looked so far away. He looked down. Did he really want to go down? He shone his flashlight downward again. Bits of glistening white flashed at him. What were they?

"What's that white stuff down there?" Jackson asked the rat.

The rat shrugged. "Bits of this and that." And he licked his nose.

And Jackson shuddered.

They were bones.

The rat chuckled. "We aren't as tidy as we like."

Jackson needed to get out of there. Like, now. He put the flashlight in his bag, gripped the toilet-paper rope, and began climbing. He made it four feet and then fell.

"Whoopsies!" the rat called out.

How was Jackson going to get out of here?

And then he had an idea.

Jackson hadn't been lying when he said he knew a lot about knots. He was in Boy Scouts. And his dad was a high-angle rescue firefighter after all. (Oh, you didn't know? Well, it wasn't really relevant until now. Maybe the firefighter part would have been cool to know, but this story is about Jackson, not his dad.)

Jackson wound the toilet paper around his hand. Then he wrapped it around his foot and stood up. He wrapped another loop around his other foot and stood up a foot higher. He did it again with the first foot.

"Oh! Look at us! Clever, aren't we? But ..." the rat turned and sat back. He rubbed his nose with his filthy paw, his nails long and creepy. "We're getting veeeeery tired. Aren't we?"

Jackson paused. He could feel the ache in his arms. He shook his head. No, he was not tired.

"Our arms are so tired! Oh, it would be so niiiiiice to ressssst, wouldn't it?" the rat hissed.

Jackson's eyes fluttered a moment. He shook his head again. He tied another loop around his other foot.

"It would be soooo much easier to just give in, wouldn't it? Sooooo tired!" The rat's tail twitched.

Jackson was tired. Very tired.

"Yes. That's it. So sleepy."

Jackson just wanted to go home.

The rat read his mind. "Yesss. We could take you home. No need to climb all the way up."

Jackson looked up. It was very, very far away. He could just drop and let the rat take him home.

"Of course, we know the way. We always know the way," the rat whispered.

Jackson nodded. That would be much easier. Then he wouldn't have to climb all the way up. Jackson let himself fall back with a jerk.

"Perfect. We'll just reach out and ..." A claw wrapped itself tightly around Jackson's arm. He was so sleepy.

"Ouch. Too tight," he murmured.

"So sorry." Jackson felt himself being pulled.

Which Has the Distinct Smell of Stimple

Jackson's nose twitched. He shook his head. He smelled ... Stimple? He sniffed again. It was the distinct smell of Stimple's garbage bag. Stimple was going to get him home.

Home!

Jackson jerked back. The rat lost his grip, and Jackson swung away.

And that was just enough time for Jackson to snap out of it.

On the swing back, Jackson's head cleared. The huge, slimy rat was standing up on its hind legs, its front claws reaching out for him. The rat's pink nose twitched and his mouth opened wide, showing off his long, yellow teeth. Jackson had only an instant to react.

Jackson pumped his weight, as if he were on a swing, and turned himself so he'd be feet first. He only had one shot.

Jackson kept his eyes open to make sure he hit the target.

With a sickening thud, Jackson's feet hit the rat right in the face, narrowly missing his wide-open jaws. The rat squeaked and fell over. Jackson began spinning backward.

"Don't play nice, do we?" The rat rubbed his nose angrily.

Jackson slowed himself from spinning and immediately began making loops around his feet to climb. One foot. The next foot. Another step.

"Nasty thing! We are not finding much patience anymore!" The rat got up and began pacing.

Jackson had climbed five feet.

"Looking especially delicious, we are!" the rat cried out. His grabby claws reached out to snatch Jackson but missed.

Jackson climbed another five feet. He felt like he could climb anything.

"Getting so sleepy!" the rat called out in his hypnotic voice.

Jackson ignored it. He was getting out of there.

"Come back! So lonely, we are!" The rat's voice was even further away.

Jackson grabbed the sharp edge of the precipice and hauled himself over, the broken edge scratching and squishing and poking his stomach.

Jackson collapsed onto his back, breathing heavily. His stomach hurt, his arms hurt, and his chest

hurt. He pulled up his shirt. Two thick, red lines criss-crossed his body, oozing blood. He curled up in a ball, trying to calm down. He closed his eyes, and made himself breathe slowly and evenly.

Jackson listened for the rat. He didn't hear anything.

He turned, pulled out his flashlight, and shone it down the canyon, down to the ledge where the rat was lurking. Two red eyes glowed up at him.

chapter 78

In Which Our Hero Takes a Deep Breath

The puddle of water was still glistening, still hanging in the air.

Jackson looked across the canyon. Could he maybe throw the roll of toilet paper across and have it catch on something and spin around, making a perfect knot, and then he could tie the other end to a branch and shimmy across? Hmm.

Jackson grabbed the roll of toilet paper and held on to the end with one hand. With the other hand, he aimed and threw the roll as hard as he could. It flew across the canyon, across a root, and fell to the ground. He pulled on the toilet paper to bring it back, but the roll caught on a rock and began to unravel. *Oof.*

Jackson stood up. He looked at the canyon. He looked at the other side. He looked back at the elevator. His mind was reeling, but a thought kept popping up in his head. Maybe, just maybe.

Jackson stepped to the edge of the cliff. He could hear a quiet snickering from far below. He stared straight ahead and took a deep breath. He put his flashlight away and adjusted his satchel, pulling the strap tighter. He cleared his throat. Nothing would stop him from falling. No harness. No safety net. No doubt.

He took a step.

chapter 79

In Which Our Hero Does Not Vomit. Not Quite.

Jackson felt the wind rushing past his face, blowing dirt and debris into his eyes. It was hard to breathe because he was falling so fast. He spread his arms out to slow down.

THUMP.

Jackson opened his eyes carefully. He wiggled his arms and legs. Stiff, but okay. He got to his feet and looked around. He was exactly where he was before, right at the top of the cliff.

What?

Behind Jackson was the elevator door with no buttons. In front of him was the other side of the canyon, still thirty feet away. Then he looked down.

And almost threw up.

chapter 80

In Which Water Behaves Very Oddly (Part II)

He saw nothing but darkness and a pair of red eyes. What was he standing on? He looked down carefully at his feet. He was on top of the glistening puddle.

Jackson reached into his bag and pulled out the nearly empty water bottle. He took a good look at it. It was a clear bottle with a blue label and white writing. It said:

LIVING WATER
Use only in emergency.

Jackson just stared at it. He supposed this situation constituted an emergency. He lifted one foot and gingerly brought it down beyond the puddle's edge. His foot went below the puddle, nearly making him fall.

Now what?

Jackson shuffled his feet. The puddle moved with them. He shuffled his feet more, dragging them toward the other side of the canyon. The puddle followed him, right underneath his feet. It was holding him up! With a final ungraceful shuffle, he jumped onto the far edge. Jackson bent down and touched the puddle with his finger again. The consistency had changed. It was slightly sticky now. Viscous. (*Viscous* means gooey, like a piece of stringy cheese from french onion soup.) Jackson uncapped his water bottle and stuck his sticky finger into the hole. The entire puddle slid in, and with a small splash, let go of his finger.

Jackson twisted the cap on and shook the bottle. The water inside splashed about just like regular water in a regular water bottle.

Huh.

Jackson put the water bottle in his satchel and began walking.

He came to an elevator, pushed the button, and with a whir and a churn ...

DING!

The door opened.

chapter 81

In Which Jackson is Understandably Annoyed

"Good day, sir," Sir Shaw smiled.

"Where were you!" Jackson yelled out. "You dropped me off, and you never picked me up!"

Sir Shaw looked at Jackson quietly. "I am picking you up now, sir."

Jackson shook his head. "No. No. You should have picked me up where you dropped me off. On the other side! You left me there by myself and I had to get across this huge canyon, and I fell and there was a rat waiting to eat me! I had to climb up and get across by myself!"

Sir Shaw adjusted his cuffs. "Did you get across *all* by yourself?"

Jackson's cheeks turned red. "Well, yeah. I mean no. Not exactly."

Sir Shaw watched Jackson carefully. "Did you have an adventure?"

"I suppose."

"Did you learn anything?"

Jackson glared at Sir Shaw. And then he calmed down. Because he *had* learned something, but he wasn't about to admit it. So he said nothing.

"Why do you not come in and have a cup of hot chocolate?" Sir Shaw asked. "I find that after-an-adventure is the perfect time for hot chocolate."

Inside the elevator was a bench that folded down from the wall. It looked very inviting. Jackson hesitated.

"I have whipped cream and extra chocolate sprinkles."

That was enough. Jackson stepped inside and sat down. Sir Shaw pulled out a shiny thermos and unscrewed the lid. The smell of warm, chocolaty goodness filled the air. He handed Jackson a huge mug and filled it up to the top with rich hot chocolate. He added a generous dollop of whipped cream and shook a canister of chocolate sprinkles on top. Sir Shaw sat down on a little stool and crossed his legs.

"Now tell me all about it."

In Which Jackson Experiences the Effects of Hot Chocolate with Whipped Cream and Sprinkles

Jackson couldn't remember the last time he had such a great conversation with someone. (Actually, the last time was last week and it was with his mom, but still. Good conversations are always enjoyable and should be more frequent.)

Jackson slurped the last of his hot chocolate and let out a warm, sugary burp. There are few things as comforting as a mug of hot chocolate and a kind ear.

"Sir Shaw?" he asked. "Is there any way that we can just go up? I'm so tired of the darkness and the grouchiness and the weirdness. I just want to go up. Back to the sunlight." He looked at Sir Shaw, trying to blink back the tears that were just behind his eyes. (Hot chocolate will do that to you sometimes.)

"One needs only to ask, sir," Sir Shaw smiled.

"Please? Please can we go up? To the very tippy-top of the tree where it's sunny and beautiful and I can see the sky going on forever? Where I can smell fresh air? Then I'll be ready to go home."

Sir Shaw nodded.

chapter 83

At the Very Tip-Top

With a whir and a churn ...
DING!

The elevator door opened.

"Top floor, sir," Sir Shaw announced.

Jackson backed up, his arm shielding his eyes from the bright light. The entire elevator was filled with a warmth that he could feel right down to his toes.

Jackson squinted and slowly brought his arm down.

"Have a good day, sir," Sir Shaw said.

"You know, you don't have to keep telling me to have a good day. I don't mind."

Sir Shaw smiled gently. "Ah, but I tell you to have a good day because I honestly want you to have a good day. I care whether you have a good day or not."

"Why?"

"Because I always care. Enjoy your day, sir." Sir Shaw extended his arm out toward the beauty that lay just outside the door.

An endless golden field spread out before them. Jackson took one step out of the elevator and felt *different.* He couldn't say how, exactly, except that he wasn't tired anymore. And that he didn't feel hungry anymore. And that he wasn't terribly worried about getting home anymore. He just felt ... satisfied.

His fingers ached to touch the golden grasses that shot up as high as his chest and to feel their soft, silky ends tickle his hands. But first he turned back to Sir Shaw.

"Is this place for real?" he asked.

Sir Shaw chuckled. "That depends."

"On what?"

"On whether you believe or not!"

Jackson laughed. He took another step on a path leading into the field.

"Have a good day, sir," said Sir Shaw.

"You too!" And off Jackson went.

chapter 84

In Which Our Hero Encounters a Most Unusual Tree

Jackson had already seen some pretty odd places in the tree, but this field was unlike any other. He stepped carefully, the ends of the grass tickling his fingers, arms, and legs. The smell reminded him of warm, baked bread with a touch of cinnamon and ginger. The sun was bright above his head, filling him with such a coziness that he simply could not stop smiling.

As he walked, he felt a tingling in his legs. An energy surged through him, and there was just one word in his mind: *run.* So he took a breath and ran.

His muscles were strong and made him fast. He ran as quickly as he could, his arms pumping with each stride. He felt the grasses brush against his bare skin, tickling him. He ran faster and faster. He spread his arms out like he'd just won a race and kept running. He felt like he could run forever.

As Jackson weaved back and forth through the grasses, making his own path, he noticed something glistening and glittering up ahead. It looked like ... a shimmering tree? He laughed. A tree within a tree.

He ran toward it.

As he ran, the tree came into focus, but that trick of the light—the shimmering look of the leaves—didn't change as he drew closer. And then, before he knew it, he was standing right in front of the tree. If he hadn't been so transfixed, Jackson would have noticed that his legs weren't tired at all. And that he wasn't even breathing hard. But Jackson couldn't think about anything but the tree.

The tree had thick bark, very much like a silver maple (*Acer saccharinum*), but with deep grooves like a black walnut (*Julgans nigra L*). The bark was brownish-grayish-blondish with black squiggles and the branches whorled like a white pine (*Pinus strobus L.*) (which in itself was ridiculous because this was clearly a deciduous tree). (*Whorled* means growing around in a circle and *deciduous* means that a tree loses its leaves in the winter. And you thought you weren't going to learn anything in this book!) But this tree didn't have leaves. Something else dangled on the branches.

Jackson stepped a bit closer. The silence was almost deafening. It was as if a hush had gone all over the world—as though this were a very special, secret place.

The tree shimmered with the most fantastic colors. Dazzling rainbows made of ten different kinds of reds, eleven yellows, fifteen greens, sixty-eight purples, thirty-two blues, and four oranges. As Jackson stepped even closer, he realized that the branches of the tree were filled not with leaves, but with little bits of colored glass, tied on delicately with fine copper wire. The tree began to tinkle, its colors rippling together, casting a rainbow so bright Jackson almost had to close his eyes. The tinkling stopped, and a bright amber piece of glass materialized right before Jackson's face. There seemed to be little scratches etched on it. He looked at the other pieces of glass. They all had little etchings on them too.

Some of the pieces of glass had hieroglyphics on them, some had Chinese writing on them, some had Russian writing on them, some had French writing on them, and some had ... oh! An English one!

On a piece of yellow glass, someone had etched in tiny, messy printing the words:

I pray my sister will get better.

*I pray
my
sister
would
get
better*

Jackson's brow furrowed. He looked at a piece of electric blue glass and read:

I pray my dad will get a job soon.

Were these all ... prayers? Jackson swallowed. What was this place? And what was this tree? He kept reading:

Please help me find my cat, Sneakers.

Thank you for helping me find my teddy bear.

Thank you for the rains. Our vegetables are finally growing.

I pray for a baby.

I pray for my mom's cancer to go away.

I pray we can sell our house soon.

I pray for a friend to play with at school.

I pray my dad won't die.

Jackson gasped. Was this ... a prayer tree? He heard a snort and then some laughter. Jackson looked up.

chapter

85

In Which Stimple Makes a
Monkey of Himself

Ya look ridiculous, bobbing this way and that.
Studying a tree, are ya? Crazy monkey-man!
Oo-oo-oo-eeee! Look at me! I'm a monkey!" Stimple
shook his body about and bobbed his head.

Jackson turned red. But not very red. He didn't
know if Stimple was still mad at him.

"Have you seen this tree before, Stimple?" he asked.

Stimple grunted. "I work here, don't I?" He dropped
the garbage bag off his back onto the ground.

"Isn't it amazing?" Jackson gestured grandly to the
tree and smiled.

Stimple stared at Jackson. "It's a tree."

Jackson nodded. "A *prayer* tree!"

"A what?"

"A prayer tree! Well, that's what I'm calling it. I think
this is where prayers go."

Stimple's eyes grew wide. "I have no idea what you're
talking about. This tree here is just a tree. Just like
any other tree, except that it's dead. I don't know why
they won't just let me cut it down."

Jackson stared at Stimple. "Can't you see the prayers?
All these little pieces of colored glass, the dazzling rainbows of ten different kinds of reds, eleven yellows, fifteen

greens, sixty-eight purples, thirty-two blues, and four oranges? Don't you see them?"

Stimple stuck his big finger inside his ear and waggled it about. It made very interesting squishy noises. "Boy, you've lost yer mind," he said. "Nope. Been here forever—tree's never changed. Dead is dead."

"But Stimple! It's here, it's ..." Jackson reached out to touch the glass but stopped himself. He shook his head. Why couldn't Stimple see it? Maybe he was imagining things? Jackson felt a cold breeze and he shivered. The sun had hidden behind a grayish cloud.

"Stimple, this has to be a prayer tree. All these bits of glass have prayers written on them!"

"Humph. Don't believe in no prayers."

"But prayers are answered all the time!"

"Poppycock!"

Jackson began to get frustrated. "You know, just because *you* don't believe in praying doesn't mean prayers aren't answered."

"Who told ya that nonsense? Bunch of frilly faith monkeys? I like my facts, thank you very much!" Stimple snorted.

Jackson laughed. He couldn't help it.

Stimple's face turned red. "What'er ya laughing at?"

"You live in a tree! You collect garbage from a tree!"

Stimple's nose turned red.

"There is an elevator right in the middle of the tree! There are talking chickens that wear makeup and run a beauty salon!"

Stimple's ears turned red.

"There is a guy in the root system bandaging up the roots so the tree doesn't walk away, and there are 3,486 squirrels living down there that harass his wife for peanut butter!"

Stimple's fingers turned red.

"There is a beautiful garden with a golden toilet right in the middle of it!"

Stimple's mouth snarled.

"I blew up here on a green-and-purple-striped umbrella—and you're telling me, despite all of this nonsense, that you don't believe in something as simple as prayer?"

"I can *see* everything that's here, and that's what makes it real," Stimple spluttered through gritted teeth. "Just because your mommy told you to say your prayers doesn't mean they're going to be answered!"

Jackson got very angry. "You ... are ... ridiculous!" he shouted.

Stimple's eyes turned red. In a flash, Stimple's hand tightened into a fist and he punched Jackson right in the thigh. (Yes, I know it's a ridiculous place to punch anyone, but Stimple is short, remember? Now be quiet. We're getting to the fight scene.)

In Which Stimple Is Not Actually All That Scary

Jackson had never really been in a fight before. I mean, he had fought with his sister, but you don't hit girls, *ever*, so these fights were always short-lived. His little brother had jumped on him a few times in the past, but his little brother was five. What did you expect? But Jackson had done some play-fighting with his dad, punching each other in the arm, swinging in harnesses while they kicked at each other, you know, stuff dads and sons do, so Stimple's punch didn't hurt very much. It actually shocked Jackson more.

Another punch to the thigh.

"Ow! What are you doing?" Jackson jumped out of the way.

"I am so sick of you ... big people!" Stimple kicked Jackson in the shin.

Jackson pushed Stimple backward. "Knock it off! You're being ridiculous!"

Stimple swung a fist at Jackson's chest, but Jackson jumped back. "Stop calling me ridiculous!" Stimple growled.

Jackson stuck out a foot and tripped Stimple, sending him flying to the ground with a heavy thud. "I'm calling you ridiculous because you *are* ridiculous!"

Stimple jumped up and threw himself at Jackson. They both landed on the ground, and the air was knocked out of Jackson's chest. Stimple may have been short, but he was one heavy troll. Stimple grabbed Jackson's arms and tried to pin him down. "Take that back!"

Jackson struggled underneath him. He had to get him off! "Okay, okay, I take it back. You aren't ridiculous."

Stimple loosened his hold a bit, and at that moment, Jackson kicked and did a backward somersault, throwing Stimple off. Then Jackson jumped up.

"You're not ridiculous. You're a big *baby!*" he cried.

Stimple rolled over and stood up. "That's it. You've asked for it!"

Jackson took a step back, his legs apart, his hands up, ready for the next attack.

Stimple's eyes opened wide, and his bushy eyebrows went right up into his head. He took a hold of his nose hair and began parting it to either side of his mouth. His lips slowly moved outward and he began to grin, yellow teeth and all. "Grr! Grrr!" he grrrd out of his teeth.

Jackson cocked an eyebrow. "What are you doing?"

"I'm scary! Look! A troll that smiles! Isn't it the ugliest thing you've ever seen? Aren't you terrified for your life? Look at you! You're trembling in fear!" He took a step toward Jackson.

"Are you serious? You think you're scary-looking?" Jackson slowly lowered his arms.

"Grr! Grrr! I'm a big ugly troll! Grrr! Nightmares for weeks!" He took another step toward Jackson, parting his nose hair even further.

"Ah, Stimple?"

"Grrr! What?"

"You're not scary-looking."

Stimple shook his head. "Yes, I am! Grr! I'm the most hideous thing you've ever seen! Don't you just want to leave now? Run away forever? Never see me again?"

"Um, no?"

Stimple faltered. "What do ya mean?"

"You're not that scary. I mean, some of the stuff stuck in your nose hair is a little unappetizing, but no, you're not scary. Or ugly."

Stimple's smile turned to a frown. "Well, I don't understand then."

"What?"

"That's what my mother said when she left."

"She said you were scary?"

Stimple let go of his nose hair and sat down on a rock. He put his big head in his big hands and stared at the ground.

"When she left. I asked her why. She said it was because I was so ugly and so scary-lookin'. Then she left."

Jackson walked toward Stimple. "That is an awful thing to say. I'm so sorry."

"What'er you sorry for? You didn't say it!"

"No, but you can say you're sorry by sympathizing with people you know. It makes them know they're cared for." Jackson put his hand on Stimple's head. He really, really didn't want to accidentally touch his nose hair that was now hanging off his shoulders.

Stimple snorted. "And why would you care for someone the likes of me?" He rubbed his nose with his fist.

Jackson tapped Stimple's head gently. He looked up so he didn't have to see the nose hair. "Everyone has a story, Stimple. And some people just need someone to listen to theirs." Stimple didn't say anything. He just sighed.

"Why don't you believe in prayer?" Jackson asked, using a casual voice so it didn't sound like he was prying or trying to antagonize Stimple. (*Antagonize* is when your little brother is sleeping beside you in the car and you lean over and poke him so he wakes up crying. You really shouldn't do that, because you're just teasing him in a bad way.)

Stimple sighed again. "Why should I? Never did me any good."

Jackson looked at Stimple. "You mean, you prayed once?"

Stimple said nothing. Jackson looked back at the prayer tree. All the colors were so mesmerizing ... Jackson felt a warmth fill his body. And then something caught his eye.

chapter 87

Which Explains a Great Deal

Jackson walked over to the base of the tree and found a persimmon-colored glass hidden in the grass. He leaned over and picked it up. It was cool and smooth, but the copper wire holding it was mangled and bent in a funny direction. Jackson held the glass closer so he could read it, but the etching was written in strange letters he didn't recognize. He walked over to Stimple, holding it gently in his hands.

"Is there such thing as Troll language?" he asked.

Stimple nodded quietly.

"Do you speak it or write it?"

Stimple sighed.

Jackson held out his hand, showing him the glass. Stimple sat up quickly. "Where did you get that?" he asked.

"I found it on the ground."

Stimple stared at the glass, then reached out to pick it up with his thick fingers. His bottom lip began to tremble.

"Stimple?"

"Even my prayers are rejected," Stimple whispered as tears fell onto his hairy face. "Not even my own mother wants me. And now the tree doesn't want me either. I'm awful!" Stimple clutched the glass tightly in his hands and fell on the ground, curled up into a little ball, and sobbed.

Jackson had no idea what to do. It isn't every day that one confronts a crying troll. He watched Stimple roll around on the ground, whimpering and sobbing. Bits of food were falling to the ground ... including a banana peel and a half-eaten cookie. Jackson needed to get control of the situation.

"Stimple?" Jackson said.

Stimple lost control. "BAAAAAAHHHH! No one loves me!"

"Stimple?"

"WHAAAAAAA! Not even a dumb tree!"

"Stimple!" Jackson yelled as loudly as he could.

Stimple stopped wailing. He sat up and snorted and sniffed.

"Stimple, I think ..."

Stimple snorted again, sucking the bubble of phlegm back into his body.

"Stimple. Let's be rational here."

"Wha, wha, what good's that gonna do?" he whimpered.

And then Jackson had an idea.

"What if we put your prayer back on the tree?" Jackson asked.

"But it fell off because ... because it was ... rejected like *meeeeeee!*" And Stimple continued sobbing, sounding like a transport truck flying down a highway.

Jackson sighed. "Stimple. It never hurts to try."
He held out his hand. Stimple stopped crying for a moment and looked down at his persimmon-colored glass. He slapped the glass into Jackson's hand. Jackson bent down and sat beside Stimple.

"There's just one thing though."

"Whass that?" Stimple spluttered.

Jackson paused. "I think you need to believe in it."

"Believe in what?"

"Believe in prayer again."

Stimple gave a very unpleasant snort. "Why would I do that? What good is that gonna do me? Foolish Stimple. Believing in rainbows and prayers. What a joke!"

Jackson swallowed hard, willing himself not to get angry. "Stimple, lots of prayers are answered. In fact, I think the Author answers every prayer. Just maybe not in the way you'd expect."

Stimple snorted in response.

"Just try. Please?" Jackson held out the glass to Stimple. Stimple looked at it. He grabbed it clumsily, touching Jackson with his thick, sweaty hand. Jackson surreptitiously wiped his hand on the grass beside him. (*Surreptitiously* is the way you slip your broccoli to the dog at dinner when your parents aren't looking.) Instead of the sweat wiping off, the grass decided to break off and stick to his hand. "Urg," he said.

"Whassat?" Stimple muttered.

"N-nothing. Just . . ."

"Jus' what?"

Jackson shrugged helplessly. "Just . . . believe."

Stimple looked at Jackson, his big red eyes still leaky with tears. He wiped his nose with his sleeve. He squeezed his eyes shut and squeezed the piece of glass in his hand. "This is dumb," he muttered under his breath.

"It's not going to be heard unless you believe."

Jackson looked up at the sky. It was still cloudy. Where was that sun? He looked at the tree. Why had it dropped a prayer?

Jackson stole a glance at Stimple. Stimple's face was turning red from effort. Jackson looked back up at the sky. The clouds began to move, slowly at first, but then they picked up speed. Stimple's hand was turning red. Jackson looked over at the tree again. Very delicately, it began to tinkle, the little bits of glass chiming gently together in the soft breeze. Jackson could feel it. Something in the air.

Something . . .

. . . amazing.

In Which Jackson Would Benefit from an Oven Mitt

Eeeeerrrrgh! Too hot!" Stimple threw his piece of glass down. He blew on his hands, flapping them in the air like a chicken trying to give you a make-over. Jackson looked down at the glass. The persimmon color was glowing like it was on fire. The copper wire surrounding it had straightened itself out and the words shone bright like fire.

"I think it's time, Stimple."
Jackson grabbed the hem of
his T-shirt and pulled it out
of his shorts, hiding his hand
underneath. He opened his
palm and picked up the hot
glass, his T-shirt protecting
his hand. He walked over to
the tree and hung the glass
up on a branch.

A bright, white light filled
the sky.

In Which the Road Leads Home

Jackson groaned and shook his head. He slowly opened his eyes. He was lying on something red and soft, and there were voices talking quietly behind him. He stayed where he was, listening.

"I'm not even sure if I believe it myself," said a deep, gruff voice.

"Well, seeing is believing, as you always say, sir," a polite voice replied.

"Humph. I guess so."

"And was it answered?" The elevator—that's where he was. Jackson felt the floor beneath him begin to lurch.

"Don't expect it to be. It was a little crazy. Even for a prayer."

"Anything is possible, so long as we believe," the polite voice said.

Jackson figured he had waited long enough. He yawned loudly and sat up. Stimple was leaning against the elevator wall, and Sir Shaw stood by the elevator's lever.

"Are you all right, sir?" Sir Shaw asked.

Jackson nodded. "What happened?"

"I cannot rightly say, sir. It seems one moment my elevator was empty, and the next, the two of you were inside." Sir Shaw smoothed his jacket. Jackson looked at Stimple. Stimple just shrugged.

"What was your prayer?" Jackson asked bluntly. It was a very personal question, of course, but sometimes personal questions are the most important ones to ask.

"Humph. It was so long ago, it doesn't really matter now, does it?" Stimple twiddled his nose hair nervously.

"What do you mean, it doesn't matter? Of course it matters! We found it and put it back on the prayer tree, didn't we?" Jackson protested.

"A prayer tree, sir?" Sir Shaw asked.

"Yeah! There was a huge tree in the middle of the field and it had shining glass hanging from the branches and there were all these prayers written on the glass and the sun was shining and then we found Stimple's prayer because it had fallen down and we hung it back up and then there was this bright, white light and then ..."

"Main floor, sir," Sir Shaw announced. The elevator did a little bounce and stopped.

"Main floor? What's on the main floor?" Jackson asked. With a whir and a churn ...

DING!

The elevator door opened.

Outside the doors was a green field with a path running down the middle of it. Far off in the distance, Jackson could make out some houses.

"Is this how I get home?" Jackson asked.

"Yes, sir. You did request to go home? This would be the path to take you," Sir Shaw replied.

Jackson looked at the path. He *did* have to go home. But wait ...

"Did I only have to ask to go to the ground floor to go home?" Jackson asked.

Stimple shuffled his feet. "Ya, well ..."

Sir Shaw smiled. "Perhaps then the adventure would never have happened?"

Stimple nodded vigorously. "Yah, that's right. Ya had to learn somethin'." Then Stimple looked at Sir Shaw. Sir Shaw nodded, and Stimple shrugged his shoulders. "And maybe ... maybe I was just lookin' ... fer a friend or somethin'." He looked down at his feet.

Jackson sighed. "You could have just asked, Stimple."

Stimple smiled awkwardly. "Ya, well ..."

"It is time, sir," Sir Shaw announced.

"Well, thanks for getting me home, Stimple." Jackson held out his hand to shake.

Stimple eyed the hand uncertainly. "I don't know where that hand's been," he growled.

Jackson shook his head. "I hope that your prayer is answered. Somehow. You just have to believe, you know?" Jackson patted Stimple's arm. Stimple nodded, still staring at the ground.

Jackson turned to Sir Shaw. "Thanks for everything. It was great seeing you again." He held out his hand, and Sir Shaw grasped it in his white-gloved one.

"Always a pleasure, sir. And remember ..." He ducked down to Jackson's height and looked him straight in the eye. Jackson felt a strange pull. It felt like his insides wanted to climb out of his body and climb right into Sir Shaw's arms. Jackson took a deep breath.

"Mind your roots. The Author will always help you find your way home," Sir Shaw whispered. Jackson couldn't say anything, so he nodded. Sir Shaw stood up, and the pull was gone. Jackson shook his head and stepped outside the elevator. The dirt path led toward the neighborhood, where all the houses were lined up in rows. He knew that just beyond was the road that led home.

"You know, Stimple, I lost my son a long time ago," the polite yet dignified voice said.

"Ya don't say? That's funny because I lost my dad a long time ago. Actually, I never really had a dad. Or a mom, for that matter," replied Stimple's gravelly voice.

"How interesting. I have never had a chance to be a father."

"I never had a chance to be a son."

And with a whir and a churn, the elevator door closed.

Normal.

Acknowledgements

Because I am not rich and famous yet, I only get a page to thank people. When I am rich and famous, I will demand fourteen pages to thank people and then no one will get offended.

Firstly, thank You to my God (who is so much fun to write with). Thank You for these gifts. Thank You for these blessings. Thank You for the growth. All good things come from You.

To my gorgeous hunk of a man, Danny: You are the apple to my pie; you are the blanket to my bed; you are the chai to my latte. Thanks for working so hard so I can keep writing. You're a rockstar. I love love love love love you! Thank you for Paris and New York.

To my lovely editor, Kathleen: You rock. For putting up with my endless emails and whining. For choosing eels instead of deer. Brilliant. I wish you well, girlfriend, and I wish you glittery disco balls and peppermint mochas, and I am still planning on New York at Christmas. Thanks for being a bestie. And Jacque: thank you, thank you, thank you for putting up with the insanity.

To my other besties: Burb, Gigi, Ally, NeeCee, Lulu, Zuzu, Lynne, Colleen and Suzanne. Ladies ... oh, the prayers you have prayed over me ... Thank you. I fully expect each of you to buy one hundred copies of my book so I can become rich and famous and can have fourteen pages of acknowledgments. And to the elevator man at Tiffany's: It was amazing meeting you and thank you for Sir Shaw's inspiring jobs.

To Zondervan, HarperCollins, Mike and Mark, Melissa, and Cindy: oh, the questions you answered for me! I'm so green, it's pathetic. Thank you!

To all the kids I got to meet and do presentations for: I loved seeing your happy faces and hearing your silly laughs.

To all those sweet emails I got from around the world encouraging me: Thank you. You make this writing worth the sleepless nights and headbanging and multiple latte drinking.

To anyone else I forgot: Thank you.

And finally, to my boy, my gaffer, my heart-walking-around-my-body ... Jackson? You are fantastic. I love your character and I love your heart. You are so funny, it makes me proud. Always be brave and always stick up for the little guy. Be who God wants you to be. Find your story. And thanks for telling me I'm beautiful, because I'm a girl and all girls are beautiful.

If anyone wants a letter from Jenn Kelly (as she has bought lovely stationery), she can be reached at jennkelly@jennkelly.com. She also has a website: www.jennkelly.com.

We want to hear from you. Please send your comments about this book to us in care of zreview@zondervan.com. Thank you.

ZONDERVAN.com/
AUTHORTRACKER
follow your favorite authors